SPITE HALL

SPITE HALL

▼

Jack Mauro

Writers Club Press
San Jose New York Lincoln Shanghai

Spite Hall

All Rights Reserved © 2001 by Jack L Mauro

Writers Club Press
an imprint of iUniverse.com, Inc.

For information address:
iUniverse.com, Inc.
5220 S 16th, Ste. 200
Lincoln, NE 68512
www.iuniverse.com

ISBN: 0-595-19322-6

Printed in the United States of America

For Carly Simon and James Hart

Epigraph

"The village of Gomersall...contained a strange-looking cottage, built of rough unhewn stones, many of them projecting considerably, with uncouth heads and grinning faces carved upon them; and upon a stone above the door was cut, in large letters, 'SPITE HALL'. It was erected by a man in the village, opposite to the house of his enemy, who had just finished for himself a good house, commanding a beautiful view down the valley, which this hideous building quite shut out."

-Elizabeth Gaskell, THE LIFE OF CHARLOTTE BRONTE

CONTENTS

One

In Which the Hero Enters, Spite Makes a Stand, and the Hero Falls

On the second of October in 1996, John Grigio is crossing Clinch Avenue at the corner of Gay Street, in Knoxville, Tennessee. The time is just after ten o'clock in the morning; he is on his way to Garamond's, the small restaurant he manages in the lobby of the Plaza Tower building, two blocks ahead.

He wears fawn corduroy trousers, a white Oxford shirt, a tweed jacket in autumnal shades of heather and rust, and a look of bitter resolution on his face at odds with the day, the place, and perhaps the century. He is walking to work but his countenance indicates a grander journey; he is walking to slay infidels, or at the very least to bring Christ to the Turk. No matter, the actual object. It is destiny on his face and in his path.

"Loser." This he utters carelessly as he nears the corner, passing an ordinary woman wearing an orange sweater and orange headband.

"Loser. Or prostitute." This, to underscore what would not have made sense, even had its first expression been heard, as it was intended not to be. The non-inflammatory woman so unknowingly slandered, so obliviously passing by, is merely wearing her pride in the town's football team. It is a color seen everywhere in the fall in this municipality; Volunteer orange, UT orange. Knoxville's orange.

'Road gang orange', John calls it. He says 'road gang orange' many times in the fall, and in various pitches of voice. John is not a native of Tennessee.

Then: the car enters the scene. A Buick from a time when the size of a car informed the world of its owner's mercantile wingspan had begun sailing up Clinch a few moments earlier. The Buick is a pale champagne color with a hint of blush, as is Mrs. Darwin Childress, its owner and driver. Little Mrs. Childress. She is sixty-two years old and appears to be at least twenty years senior to her actual age. She resembles and has resembled since her fifth decade a petite and wizened apple.

Little Mrs. Childress—she is not in reality quite so tiny, but is compacted, somehow, in other peoples' visions and memories—clutches the huge wheel of her car. At least two of her fingers could fit comfortably in one of its grooves, sculpted for a single digit. Her jeweled hands close together at the wheel's base, the genteel tip of her tiny tongue fractionally protruding from her little scarlet lips in exertion, she steers her car. To a Dali-esque mind she could in fact be plucked out of the Buick and be nervously airborne, so determined is her grasp on the wheel. But she sails, sails up Clinch Street, past the optometrist, past the stage door to the Tennessee Theatre. Her eyes are narrowed and already fixed on the left corner ahead, as thence will speed the traffic she must beware. A mother and son waiting in the eye doctor's office look up as she passes; the mother, within an unmapped recess of her psyche, is surprised that no local beauty queen is languidly waving from atop the Buick, so stately does the vehicle pass by. Junior senses something. He is equipped with the precognitive nose possessed by most dumb animals and some small boys.

John has peripheral vision as other people have a ready handshake. He sees the Buick. Oh, yes. Yet he does not halt or hurry his pace to allow for the nearing car's negligence. What he does, in fact, is deliberately stop and stand. In the middle of the street. His eyes narrow in defiance. Under his breath he hisses, "Come on. Oh, come *on!*" The driver, incorrectly and determinedly focused little Mrs. Childress, does not see John until the Buick has stopped, impeded in its progress by his thigh.

John's left leg is then broken. Complicated damage is as well done to his knee. He does not, however, fall. Having expected the event–having beckoned it, in fact–his posture had been as rigid as his determination. But even the most willing or willful flesh is flesh regardless, and must rely upon skeletal support. John does not fall, but he does bend. For the next few minutes, his torso will rest on the sumptuous hood of the Buick, his arms splayed over it; a wounded and grimacing parody of an infatuated buyer at a car lot.

Immediately afterward, the clumsy choreography that appears within moments of an accident transforms the corner of Gay and Clinch into a serious, but pitiably amateurish, Vaudeville stage. None of it is exceptional. The boy from the optometrist's office rushes out, hoping to see a life-sized and therefore better version of the violent content he turns to the television for. But that is what boys do.

*

Only a few other ripples in the concentric field around the aftermath of the accident–we call it that still, knowing the truth–may be considered notable. One ripple, and a substantial one at that, is Lawyer Duffy. He happens to be standing on the opposite sidewalk a moment before the collision, slightly diagonal to the scene itself, and is scarring his fat thumb with many an attempt to flare his disposable lighter into life and bring some semblance of real purpose to the puffing of his cigar. John's destiny explodes with that of little Mrs. Childress, and Lawyer Duffy may as well have a theater program stuffed into his brown serge pocket, so perfect is his view.

Two things should be made clear here: Lawyer Duffy has a Christian name. He was given one shortly after his birth sixty-five years past, as he was laden with Christian principles not long after. But the name, like

some of the principles, has been deftly pushed into the wings over time by
the more commanding occupation he has made his own. He is not uneth-
ical, nor immoral. It is more that any man who prefers to be so identified
by his trade, as Duffy does, is so deeply one with that trade that ethics and
morality are, if not extinguished, rendered immaterial. This is often the
case with love, and we wink at it then, too. So the familiar name of Duffy
is employed almost exclusively by his sister.

Moreover: Lawyer Duffy is acquainted with the Buick and its owner.
He has done in the past rather pedestrian and modestly profitable business
for Mrs. Childress. She is an ideal client: moneyed, widowed and ignorant
of all affairs legal. He is fond of her, as well. If he is fond of her because she
has ever been the perfect client, the affection is nonetheless genuine.
Affection, once on its toddler's legs, may exist independently of its sources
of origin. Yet he saw John, he saw the careful eyes of Mrs. Childress look
only to the left as her Buick neared the corner, and he saw her car break
John's leg. At that moment, his black Bic still no match for the peevish and
small gusts of wind Knoxville blows, he was drafting a brief in his gray and
bushy head. The evil thud to be heard when car and thigh met was even
then, at the precise point of its occurring, the subject of a reconstructive
and subtly restrained speech to be made before a judge. For Lawyer Duffy
already was quite sure that the young man in the tweed jacket–the man
from the restaurant?–would be lame for a very long time.

Ripple Two is called Rodney Bourne. Rodney's job largely consists of
transporting architectural blueprints from designer to bank to builder and,
when the enterprise is blessed by the second link in the chain, back to
designer. He is cycling to Titch and Pratt headquarters in the Plaza Tower
when the accident occurs. He is young, in the boy/man foliage of his early
twenties. Rodney is as well blonde, and not just blonde. He is blonde so
sinlessly, that an army of Rodneys might well overturn the poor repute
blondes carry in this world. He is freckled to boot, and his freckles never
seem to quite keep up with his Schwinn—they follow, always, a second
behind, and never quite return to their original places. He rides past the

entire scenario and sees the peculiar timing of John's crossing before the collision without truly seeing it; as we only afterward identify as a murderer the fellow who, a moment earlier, strolled behind the man who collapsed to tastelessly reveal a blade between his shoulder blades. So Rodney sees, but takes in nothing just yet. He maneuvers on Gay to skirt the legal girth of Lawyer Duffy as the thud resounds and lives are, like a needle bumped on a vinyl recording, switched into grooves out of their ordained syncopation.

If everything stemming from a ripple stayed neatly rippling, things would be perfectly fine for Rodney. But life devises geometric variations to render ripples insultingly uncomplicated. Rodney will need every freckle to come through what the widening of his own carries him to.

There is no actual third ripple. There is, however, Andrea. Andrea Cornell. She is smoking a cigarette on the corner of Cumberland and Gay, just diagonally across the street from the misadventure. She is on the short side, on the pretty side, and never, ever on any other side but her own. She is employed as a server at Garamond's and is at the time of the accident running late. She smokes hurriedly before crossing to the Plaza Tower, entering the restaurant and, five minutes later, sitting with another cigarette and a nice hot coffee. She is aware of the calamity a block away but ignorant of its involving her manager. And, as Lawyer Duffy's trained synapses had sparked into being for their owner the legal consequences of the accident at the moment of its happening, so too does the smaller, less judicial, but far more intricate brain of Andrea spring into action. John's upper person is not yet temporarily flared out on the hood of Mrs. Childress' Buick when Andrea begins calculating how the trauma of having witnessed the horror may be adapted to ease her work day. This is mentally rung up and pocketed by her before her sneaker completes an indistinctly sinister grinding of her cigarette butt on the sidewalk.

Not on the scene, but deserving of ripple rank: Miss Louisa Duffy, the sixty-ish ingenue sister of Lawyer Duffy, dressing for a luncheon date set for two hours hence. Her reliably avuncular brother had arranged it and, even as Miss Duffy runs a brush through her waves of stone gray hair, like a ship riding a darkly stormy sea, she knows it will be a fruitless encounter. Her brother has no idea as to the sort of man she most yearns for, nor of the obscenely brief period of time she would like to share with such a man. She would tell Randolph Duffy, but she sincerely believes that the information would kill him. She is almost right. So her deep ache goes unvoiced for many years and she dines with many surpassingly wrong men, because she loves her brother and does not wish to be the instrument of his death.

Absent also from the vortex of the scene, yet inexorably one with it: Bob, hospital intern, dizzyingly good looking, at that time at his job and awaiting his own destiny, just as too handsome men do on daytime television; Mrs. Ellen Ansley, bosom friend and unsolicited bodyguard to Ruth Childress, then scanning her newspaper in the stark comfort of her home, searching for inadvertent slurs in the living section against those of her seniority; and Miss Marchbanks. Miss Marchbanks, behind the reception desk of Gilley, French and Sweet on the Tower's 20th floor. It is as well that she has no window from which to survey the hubbub at street level. A finger twirls in her hair, the telephone rings, and her concentrative powers are then stretched to their limit. Before the phone is answered. On this day, we have Miss Marchbanks on the 20th floor as a dimwitted and beribboned spirit, or lesser angel, high above the strange scene of John's collision with Mrs. Childress. It is questionable if she is ever had by anyone as more.

Lastly: fifteen minutes later and deep within the hollows of the Plaza Tower, Rene Dacres hears what happened. She is John's subordinate at Garamond's only in the strictest hierarchal sense; she is the closest thing to what the world calls a friend in John Grigio's possession. Duffy himself stops by to inform her at the small restaurant, where she has in fact been wondering about the normally punctual John's failure to appear.

Rene is troubled by the news. She is not moreover even free to examine or give vent to her disquiet, because of Andrea. There was something perverse in Andrea's breathless recounting of the accident she had been near to, minutes before. Learning now that her boss was the victim in it creates in Miss Cornell a deviant merriment at being so selected by Fate for extra inclusion in the day's upheaval. Had Andrea been present at the storming of the Bastille, the event might well have reached future generations as a day in which she passed by a noisy prison and broke a heel.

Rene cannot just now abide the young woman's egocentric take on an accident still inadequately explained to her. Furthermore, that she knows nothing of John's current condition is distressing. She sends Andrea home. Who is not entirely inhuman, for she is genuinely grateful today for her good fortune.

Rene calls Sterling Realty. Alice Ann, the aunt with whom she lives, answers. Rene tells her of what has occurred and indicates the possibility that her day may take a new and longer direction.

"Oh, that poor man," Alice Ann says.

"I should be home before you anyway. But I didn't want you to worry, if I wasn't."

"Oh. *Honey.* I understand."

Alice Ann Dacres hangs up the telephone and shoots rapid looks at various points within the confines of Sterling. She likes this not at all. She wants to be able to walk over to Carolyn and discuss this fresh evidence of her niece's folly. As Carolyn would only stare blankly at her in response, she remains behind her desk, disliking John Grigio. If he is not homosexual, he is, to her mind, even worse.

Lawyer Duffy, lifeless cheroot in his mouth, was quite correct in his appraisal of the accident. John Grigio will in fact walk with a limp in that leg for the rest of his life. After the dust of the scene had settled and lawyers, Duffy and otherwise, had done for each side what lawyers do, John found himself the owner of a good story gone to waste, as he had little use for social ploys of an anecdotal order, and a small house with a gargoyle above the door. While this—the house, not the granite demon—was an unpremeditated result of his choice in stopping in the middle of the avenue that morning, he never saw it as a stroke of fortune arising from a calamity. He would not have regretted what he had done, the sudden and madly implacable determination to spite the driver of the car, if there had been no consequence save the limp. If a man can limp proudly, he did so. His limp was his trophy, the manifestation of what he saw as his rightful, and righteous, spite.

Two

Involving Italian Coffee, and Scenes Both Exterior and Internal

It is the second week of November of 1996, a year to be recalled in Knoxville as one in which winter made an almost spitefully vehement and early arrival. The town, taken unawares by sleet in late October, takes it very personally as well, and talks about the weather amongst itself as soldiers discuss a surprise enemy move. In broken sentences, absolutely incessantly, and with more than a little admiration.

At nine-thirty in the morning of this day, Rene Dacres asks a customer entering Garamond's if it is snowing outside. The restaurant, set in the mall-like alley of shops at the rear of the Plaza Tower, managed professionally and not a little paternally by John Grigio, has no windows to the outside world, no exposure to the street. In warmer weather this is accepted by Rene; a mere handful of hours prevents her from enjoying the spring, and she is too diligent of her work to lament that necessary delay. But winter storms disrupt business, and the likelihood of a disastrously slow day is exacerbated by its cause remaining unseen and unknown by her. So she asks the few people stopping in. As she asks, now, Kelly Clifton-Cass, buxom seductress of the Knoxville advertising world.

"The garage is pretty empty, too", Kelly says, waiting for a double espresso.

Rene is thoughtful. She twists the wrench-like coffee holder into place and switches on the water; steam hisses like an unseen and very small demon. Rene is twenty years old, with short brunette hair and a round, unpretentiously pretty face. The clarity of her hazel eyes, the pleasing curves of her fair cheeks, the careless fringe of a careless chestnut bang, form an exterior pleasingly and accurately reflective of the soul behind it, and life would be a far simpler affair if all appearances were as faithful an indication of all wholes. Her figure is good as well, and both men and women alike are usually at a loss as to how to assess her nice looks; they are indisputably there, but it is hard to say whether the soft intelligence of her expression impedes or enhances her appeal. Her gaze is never hard, but it is sometimes searching. Whatever gives her eyes life gives them weaponry, too. There are those not comfortable with potential behind pretty eyes.

"As a matter of fact", Kelly continues, "I should've stayed home. *No one's* coming in, I'll bet." She holds two sugar packets and gently shakes their contents down, preparatory to adding them to her coffee. Kelly likes Rene; she likes coming into Garamond's every day, likes chatting briefly with her. Rene is clearly not of a low character or class, as one might take a waitress to be. As those not waitresses most particularly take waitresses to be. Moreover, Kelly perceives that Rene looks up to her a bit, as the supremely confident and successful young businesswoman she is. It is agreeable to Kelly to be thought of in this way; as, perhaps, a role model.

Rene seals the lid over the steaming cup and takes Kelly's money. There is in fact no single thing about Kelly which stimulates Rene's reverence. But part of Rene's appeal to that woman, and to much of Garamond's clientele, is an inherently well-bred disposition to reflect desires expressed, as do mirrors in the better clothes shops. When in actuality Rene Dacres has given thought to Kelly Clifton-Cass, it is framed in sympathy for her overly ample chest and for the somewhat ridiculous trio of hard sounds in her name.

Change is returned and, as always, Kelly leaves a dollar on the counter. She holds her coffee but does not immediately leave. Instead she says: "I'm thinking. If I just turned around now and went back to my car, no one'd know."

Rene smiles and raises her eyebrows, a wholesome conspirator. "You *could...*"

"You'd keep my secret?"

"Oh, that's silly!" Rene places her small, exquisitely white and incongruously unblemished hands on her hips, and Kelly immediately and intuitively sees this gesture as an inheritance from a mother.

How impossible are we, to think we can know things? The parental hands on hips taken in and adopted by Rene had belonged to her father.

"For one thing, who else is coming in today?" Rene adds. "For another, John may send *me* home."

Kelly pushes her bosom forward by an inch, as Spain once claimed the Low Countries. It is for her a reflex triggered by any news. For John and what he had done on Clinch Avenue is still, if not a hot story, keeping warmly on a back burner. It was during John's benign incarceration at Baptist Hospital that the tale spread and mutated, six weeks before. But the evolving nature of the story itself, the allure of the as yet indefinably disordered as having been in local action, saves it from the fate of being labeled as yesterday's mashed potatoes. Craziness dressed well is a tree perennially bearing the fruit of gossip.

"He's here? Since when?" Neither Kelly nor her bosom even attempt to cloak her surge of interest.

"Last week. There's problems with the leg or he'd have been in before that."

What is between the two women now is a thing not unfamiliar to Rene, although she has yet been unable to fully understand it. It is a duel of sorts; the customer at Garamond's wanting to remark perhaps unkindly, or at least uncomprehendingly, of John Grigio's notorious action, and Rene delicately combining a friendly receptivity to anything the customer may care to relate with an undercurrent of protection. Somehow, tacitly, the people who come to Garamond's and ask about John have the sense that jokes or disparagements will not be welcome. And Rene feels that they are holding back, and holding back because of something they feel from her. On a level she has not examined, this gives her satisfaction.

So Kelly pulls in just a little. Her breasts step back. Joking, conjecture, can wait till she gets to the office of Grange and Bailey Advertising, on the twelfth floor of the Tower. It is probable that none of her colleagues yet knows that John Grigio is there, in the building once more. She can now ascend to her office with both espresso and anecdotal gold. An Olympian handmaiden in Donna Karen.

"Nothing too bad, I hope? I mean, the leg's been *set*, right?"

Rene moves her head back and forth in a gesture of ignorance, her short bangs swaying in the movement. "I honestly don't know. It's been set too *long*, really. That cast should be off by now. Something's not right."

Kelly Clifton-Cass will later relate this conversation to several people at Grange and Bailey, and she will draw special attention to the stamina with which she withheld comment at this juncture. She will say, 'Something not right, all right', and elicit laughter. The men in attendance will even appreciate the joke as a bonus to the direct ogling of her chest the telling of it will momentarily provide. But all Kelly says now is, "Well, I'm sure it'll be fine. You take care, now."

Rene echoes the sentiment to Kelly's departing figure. Neither woman knows that, in the few minutes since Kelly left her car on level three of the Plaza Tower parking garage, the snowstorm drastically increased in strength. Kelly will negotiate her way on the icy streets less than thirty minutes later; fifteen minutes after that, she and her vehicle will be demurely propped in a ditch on Kingston Pike. The famous bosom will bear imprints of car wheel for hours after her rescue.

Rene will stay in Garamond's a short while longer. With John.

*

Whom we look at now, alone, in the elevator-like confines of Garamond's office. The space is cramped, but we will not stay long.

John Grigio would be highly displeased to know that he was under any sort of scrutiny, just then. Before the accident he would have had no such bias. Months later, armed with the cane he would use for the rest of his life, a breezy equanimity would be within him as well; the world could look to its vulgar and global heart's content. The walking stick would exist as an elegant prop and in fact draw more, and more deserved, attention to the correctness of the Grigio exterior. But now, in a monstrously large cast, the disruption to appearances is too great. His leg is a circus. It promises a story to greedy eyes with which the rest of he, arms and head and torso and unwounded leg, cannot hope to compete.

Let there be no misapprehension: John was not beautiful. Nor was he in any way deluded by notions of beauty not within, or around, his being. What he was, was perfect. That is to say, he had approximately three surface layers of perfectness at his disposal, one always at the ready to be witnessed should one or the other fail.

In what resided this perfectness? John was thirty-four years of age in 1996, which is as close to a perfect age as our species gets. That he was not a masculine ideal of beauty enhanced, rather than weakened, his second perfectness, that of his form. For John was the sort of nice-looking man Hollywood directors want on film, and then rashly and mistakenly hire pretty actors to impersonate. John's face could be on occasion handsome, but it was never not agreeable in aspect. His height was an excellent inch below the perhaps showy bar of six feet. His weight was such that, had he been a woman, he would have been hated by other women for it. He even belonged to a gym and used the equipment there to sculpt a passable silhouette, and thusly add a little muscle to one aspect of his contempt for his fellow creatures. And his Mediterranean ancestry imbued his features with dark brush strokes of humanity. This is what we know as nice-looking and, to the canny possessor of it, it is better than beauty.

Then we move to that appearance which is not appearance at all, but is inextricably one with it: the animated John, the speaking and moving Grigio. John had done his homework as a boy. He had believed that the adult world was peopled with sophistication and grace, and he had lost no time in assimilating as much of these qualities into his physicality as a small boy can. Which is, really, quite a lot. Both very young and younger John watched many old movies. It was not lost on him that even second-ary characters looked good carrying parcels across from the streets the stars trod, that even unimportant scenes could be spoken in such a way as to make them worthier of notice. He believed in his heart that it was every person's responsibility to look and move and talk as they did in those movies. He that could not should stay at home, inside.

This, the tertiary perfectness of John, had been achieved by his twen-ties. Speech was deepened through the dangerous cosmetic of cigarettes, and an already low baritone was given more color. Archness and preten-sion—to be avoided, at all costs— had been whittled away in the teen years. The best dancers are clumsy at the first rehearsals; John's adolescence had been years of rehearsal. What remained in adulthood, then, was the balance he had sought, the thousands of small smiles combined with hun-dreds of head turns and dozens of looks, alternately amused, quizzical, exasperated or imperious. The combinations were not endless, but it was a rich catalogue for the span of a lifetime.

We look at John now, then, all that perfectness lodged uncomfortably in a tiny office in the rear of a small restaurant in an office building in the city of Knoxville. Rene is in the restaurant still. Andrea is of course long gone, having executed an alternating series of doubts as to the likelihood of any business coming their way with masterfully false expressions of a desire to stick it out. If John does not leave the office shortly, Rene will knock to inform him of what is transpiring in the frightened town around them. She will call his cab from the lobby's security desk and wait for it with him, the two locked in separate reveries, staring at the hypnotic and astonishingly thick cascade of flakes falling beyond the glass front of the Plaza Tower.

It is perfectly natural that Rene should so easily visualize the next hour of the day. People who work together closely and in a regular routine frequently develop and enjoy the nicest parts of the union of marriage, and are faced with none of the messy ones. They come to feel and depend upon the unalloyed support of each other, yet engage in none of the histrionics to be seen when love is expected and not always in evidence. There is the warmth of souls in collaboration, and neither gets—perhaps subconsciously—hit in the back in the middle of the night.

John makes his tortured way out of the office. He has learned that, by resting his back temporarily against the side of the cigarette machine, he can lock up with minimal fumbling. He both appreciates and resents each small trick attained, as the weeks in the cast pass and the stench, to him, becomes ever more intolerable.

He emerges into the main space of Garamond's at a propitious moment: Rene is in fact awaiting his entrance, assured in the mostly silent understanding they share that he will soon present himself to give the order she anticipates, to close up the café. He stands supported by the beams of his crutches and notices immediately, with the house-counting eyes of a true restaurant person, that all is in readiness for a shutdown. Rene looks at him and sees his gaze dart melodramatically to the left, to the right, then to her.

"Andrea?" he inquires.

"What do you think?" Rene replies. "About fifteen minutes after she came in."

"What a trooper," John sarcastically remarks, then hops to the counter. Then a figure pulling open the door arrests both their attentions. Rene automatically defers to John, to utter to this representative of the world his decision.

"Ah…I'm sorry. We're closing up."

Their visitor is Rodney Bourne. Rene recognizes him and innocently misapprehends his purpose in stopping by.

"Hi. Were you looking for Andrea?"

"*No.*" This is delivered with a force usually not in keeping with a simple disavowal. "No. I just thought you were open. But it's no big deal." Rodney smiles at the two of them, and John and Rene, again in the solidarity of their working relationship at Garamond's, both observe a pleasantly concentrated scrutiny in the boy's regarding of the two of them. He stares, but as one raptly looks upon a place or person of which the reality had been questionable. There is palpable relief of some kind in his eyes and easy smile. Then he raises one palm in a good-natured farewell, and turns and goes.

"Nice kid," John says.

"Yes," Rene answers quickly. Very quickly. A 'too bad that...' is careening around the front of her mind. But she contains it until the unvoiced concern dies the unexpressed death such thoughts are heir to.

"Let's get out of here," John advises.

Reggie, the cook, had been sitting on a large pot in the rear of the small kitchen, out of sight and actually there in only the most temporal way. He is relatively new to Garamond's, yet has been already enveloped by the mutual intuition of John and Rene. Neither needs to outright tell him that he may go home; neither needs, in fact, to address him at all. As the barest nod informs the dog that his master deems it time for an excursion, so is Reggie preternaturally alert to the signals of his release. Someone's keys jingle, and Reggie is halfway to the parking garage.

Rene moves deftly to tuck in the last vestiges of the closing procedure. Her hand on the light switch, she asks: "Are you seeing Dr. Perkey today?"

The pair perform the ritual of the bolting of the main door. John looks around him at the corridor of the Plaza mall, losing its last inhabitants as though to the squeal of an air raid siren. "I don't think," he says, "anyone is seeing anybody today."

*

The cab summoned by Rene arrives sooner than any Knoxvillian would think possible, seeing, as John and Rene see, the ballet gone wrong of people gliding on freshly slick sidewalks. There is time, then, to note only one thing more about Mr. Grigio. It is under the first and second and third layers of John. It is beneath the rage he displays now and again, to no one or to someone like Rene.

He has never forgiven the world for being human.

*

What he does, in fact, is deliberately stop.

Why did John stop in the middle of the street, on that October day? Why did he choose, literally choose, to bring on a calamity easily avoided by a minimally increased hurrying of his steps?

The answer is simple. As John's left foot had touched upon the pavement of Clinch Street, its fellow still poised on the curb, his head had turned. As heads very often turn, to gauge in an urbanly feral way that time will permit a safe, if just a bit hurried, crossing. But John's eyes, not unexpectedly lodged within his turning head, had seen the eyes of Mrs. Childress, behind her car's windshield. And what he had seen in them was a resolve not in keeping with sweet old ladies, but one more to be associated in the mind with rabid adherents of one faith busily piling up logs for the warm extermination of another. He saw a blind purpose in the direction of her gaze he had seen many times before on the faces of other drivers; a single-minded preoccupation with what vehicles may be coming from the left, at the intersection just ahead. With no thought whatsoever to the possibility, the ridiculously distinct possibility, that a person may indeed be in the process of walking to the other side.

It is hard to say when a man's moment arrives. Some never do, or do and remain stranded because the human instruments of them are sort of out-of-town when the Fates point their fingers and call. Some occur but go unrecognized as such, because the witnesses at the scene are incapable

of seeing them. Some are seen and dismissed because, although momen-
tous in nature as such moments must be, they are a shade too complicated
and belong to no readily identifiable genre of heroism. And all that are
seen are seen only after the fact. At least, by those who document such
things. Scribes, recorders, people with no moments.

This was John's, on the second of October in 1996. He saw that Mrs.
Childress was not going to see him, that she was proceeding as so many
other careless drivers have proceeded and will proceed, that she would
blindly look to the only space with which she was concerned. So John
made, both literally and metaphorically, his stand. The knowledge that
within seconds he would be in great pain was with him, as was the tingling
unease just below the scalp when we know we are choosing to do something perhaps insane. But spite had its way. Spite was in John's blood, a
restless coagulant, a bastard strain of a noble house. John as a Grigio was
Italian. That he was born American may explain this diluted form of
revenge flowing through his veins. For spite is revenge with water liberally
stirred in. Thus did he freeze, and stand, and wait the eon of the two seconds it took for the fender of the Buick to be confronted by his left leg.

That is why John deliberately stopped.

Three

A Stay at the Hospital, with Visitors Medical, Legal, Social and Hallucinatory

We remain in that fateful week in October, a little longer. We open the curtain on our hospital scenario, equipped with both requisite misery and handsome intern.

Two days after the encounter between the Childress Buick and the Grigio leg, John was in room 232 of Baptist Hospital. He did not know what wing he was in, if it was in fact a wing he occupied. He had not been conscious when brought in; there had been a farcically sadistic moment in the ambulance when a hulking paramedic had poked the tip of his finger at John's thigh, heard John scream, and smiled. But John could not be sure this had really transpired. And there was no recollection of exiting or entering anything of a substantially different scenic character thereafter. Since being admitted, his only excursions beyond the door of room 232 had been brief and excruciating trips on wheels down a short stretch of corridor to another door. Which opened to the world, or at least to a detail of its Knoxvillian landscape, and from whose other side a cigarette could be smoked.

There was much he did not then know. The past two days had been a textbook case of the peculiar things that happen within a person following a not fatal accident. He sleeps confusedly and too deeply on medication and awakens to surroundings he does not know, each time he awakens. The seductive pleasures to be had in such a circumstance, and they do exist, particularly for the reflective sort, are countered by strikes of prosaic and extraordinary pain. Flashes of sense steal upon him in repose and he recalls and knows everything, including that elusive fact of who he is, and are then shuffled aside by dreamy speculations on the likelihood of lying on that bed forever. One's own fingers become hypnotically deserving of sustained scrutiny. Then reality—as, again, pain—intrudes like a heavy footstep on the ceiling above. And nothing is more desired than to get out.

In the late afternoon of this second day, John was as composed as he would be in that place during the five-day duration of his time there. He had not come to terms with his spitefully self-damaging action, in the hours his mind replayed the footage. Nor had he had an epiphanic reversal of sensibility regarding the old woman. He had not even yet acknowledged her in his thoughts by name; she was 'the silly old bitch'. God had not entered John's heart, calamity had not changed his bilious soul. He was composed because he had just had a cigarette.

Yet this is not damning to him, that humanity may be perceived in John simply because a base desire has been gratified. It must be noted that he was actually and simply grateful for the chance to smoke he had finagled from a softhearted intern; he was truly happy that he had been allowed this minor luxury, in the face of the catastrophe to his life waiting inside his kneecap and outside the Baptist Hospital room. To compound the spite of John Grigio with other vices, with smallness of character, may seem a logical progression, or even a natural impulse. But it would be an injustice. If spite is bad, it is bad enough. There is no need to peruse further the archive of human failings.

The intern's name was Bob. John knew that and little else. Bob, as seen by the supine John, was a very odd sort of person. For one thing, he was far too good looking for so backstage a job. Bob's face was a cubist painting, all angles and promontories of cheekbone, framed by masses of embarrassingly glossy black hair; "Got to be Irish...", John had mumbled sleepily upon being returned by Bob to his adult-size crib. Unexpectedly gentle in transferring John from the wheelchair to the bed, Bob had heard this observation as a misplaced order for a specific type of alcohol and unthinkingly attributed it to medication. Which was a solid half of a correct analysis.

"Man," the intern had said when he transported John to the chair for the first illicit outing, and said each time he so conspired with John, "You must need to smoke *bad.*" In a sense, Bob was a spiteless and beautiful version of John himself. He too was largely removed from the world and primarily an observer of its antics. That someone would so long for a cigarette as to endure an unnecessary resurgence of agony amazed him. Thus he, Bob, took care to move John as slowly and as painlessly as possible.

Once, in a waking dream brought on by a syringe the size of a small oxygen tank to his right buttock, John entertained the possibility that this intern did not in actuality exist. It seemed more likely that his mind had fooled itself into believing his craving had been satisfied, than that a stranger had been kind. Then he slept deeply and saw the face of Mrs. Childress. In the dream her eyes were on him, and she was smiling. She also stepped on the gas.

*

Day four. Baptist Hospital and John Grigio were partners in an uneasy truce. He had in fact done nothing in the way of demanding behavior, but the nurses are seasoned. They know a potential button-pusher when they see one. John in turn could read the wariness in the wholesome expanses of their open eyes. He could hear it below the soft and absolutely empty phrases they spoke. He knew the ammunition of pain killers and food was theirs to wield or withhold. Then there was the very real possibility that a white-shod foot would daintily stomp down on those few and blessed trips to the outside door theretofore winked at.

So John's irritation at small things gone wrong, gingerly layered over his outrage at his condition, remained internal and unvoiced. Only the walls of room 232 took in a 'angel of mercy, my ass', or a 'stupid, *stupid* woman'. And even then in a hushed tone. But his room would not betray him. Hospital walls, if ever they boasted the metaphoric ears we slap on other walls, are likely deaf from abuse. Or unwilling to take in anything further, having heard far too much.

Day four. At twenty minutes past five in the afternoon, the door opened and someone wearing real shoes and non-disposable clothing slipped in. It was Lawyer Duffy.

He entered and said, "Well. Well, now. How *are* you, son?" John's lips parted to frame a reply when he saw Duffy remove his chart from the foot of the bed. And seemingly scan it. John's lips remained separated from one another, but nothing issued forth. He was temporarily and mildly dumb-founded. He knew Duffy's legal calling. Duffy was a semi-regular at Garamond's. Duffy purchased lightly but tipped decently, so Duffy was not completely abhorrent to John. And here was Duffy. Reading his chart.

"Mr. Duffy." This John said, both to confirm the reality of what was a rather unreal moment and to retrieve the old man's attention.

"John, John," answered his guest, still not looking in his direction, still examining the chart.

So singular a situation allowed for almost any comment at all, or so it seemed to John.

"Can I...*help* you, Mr. Duffy?" The reversion to a question familiarly asked by him at the restaurant was not perhaps the most apt or pithy sentence to be formed. But it was something. As it turned out, it was just what was needed. Duffy slipped the clipboard back on its hook and faced the man he'd come to see. At last.

"I'm glad you said that, John. Now, the thing is, I'm here to help *you*."

One of several good things about Lawyer Duffy is that his Southernness is not smarmy. It is not waved about like the calling card it's often used as by lawyers or salesmen or by the many Southerners employed in such predatory careers. It is there, certainly, and as resolutely there as Duffy's bushy eyebrows and portly carriage. But Mr. Duffy does not inflate it. Mr. Duffy does not stress or rely too heavily upon anything showy at all. It may be that, early in life, he chose a path of understatement, having realized that he was not cut out to be of the commanding legal breed who draw applause from jurors.

A small thing, this understatement of Southernness, for which John is grateful.

"Have you spoken to an attorney yet, John?" Lawyer Duffy is also not one to waste time, or billable hours.

No. John had not. John had spoken only to doctors whose names he didn't know, a few wide-eyed nurses with suspicion in their hearts, and the kind and angular Bob. And Rene, who belonged to his regular life and therefore didn't, under the circumstances, count.

At this point Lawyer Duffy pulled a canvas chair up to the side of John's bed. For the next fifteen minutes he spoke plainly to John of what, as far as he knew it to be, the situation was. He outlined the usual procedures following such an accident; he mentioned his acquaintance with little Mrs. Childress–he even employed the diminutive adjective–and informed John of that lady's eagerness to put things right. He spoke confidently of the generosity of her insurance.

Everything Mr. Duffy said and the way in which he said it had a marvelous effect on John. It didn't bring him back into the world, but it opened up the vista to it lately concealed. As gracefully as Bob shepherded John from bed to chair, and wheeled him out of room 232 for cigarettes. But something seemed unclear. Actually, the crux of the matter, what would be taken as the cause for the visit itself, was vague.

"Mr. Duffy—"

Who waited to be inquired of as peacefully as a tranquil Santa Claus.

"Mr. Duffy, I'm sorry if I'm being stupid…"

"Not at all, not at all," interjected Duffy, taking for granted the converse.

"…but are you *with* Mrs. Childress? Are you her lawyer?"

"You could say that, John. You could say that."

Can't anyone south of Pennsylvania, John wondered, just answer a question?

"But we don't think this is a real complicated situation, son."

"Mrs. Childress and yourself?"

"Well, yes. Mrs. Childress and myself. You could say that. Although, John, others are involved. Naturally enough." Duffy then raised his plentiful hindquarters a bit, reached between his legs for the edge of his seat, drew it forward, moved, crablike, with it, and redeposited himself closer to the upper portions of John. This increased propinquity being of an insufficient degree, Duffy inclined his frame forward. So that his nose, bushy eyebrows and breath fragrant with tobacco and mint were within inches of John's own, almost startled face.

"Do you know the lady, John?" This struck John's ears, in suavity of tone and suggestiveness of delivery, as pimpish.

"Mrs. Childress? Ah…no, sir. I don't believe I do." A hundred movies from the past triggered in John an instinctively non-committal stance. He would reveal nothing, and assuredly not reveal it to the counsel for the silly old bitch.

"A fine woman. A *fine* woman." A purple hat, thought John. A big purple hat on Duffy, and some visible gold in his fillings, and the picture would be complete.

"I don't doubt that, Mr. Duffy."

"Then I surely don't need to tell you, son, she feels just terrible about this. Terrible, terrible. She talked of coming by here, but I thought it best to see you myself. First."

"I understand." Not understanding it at all, John had the fleeting impression of Mrs. Childress shyly entering his room. He had not really seen her, yet see her, then, he could.

Lawyer Duffy suddenly and simultaneously stood and pushed his chair back. This surprising agility removed the brief phantasm in John's mind and replaced it with one of the now erect Duffy thrusting his forefinger in his face. Which did not occur.

"Well, I done that." In essence, the forefinger of Duffy *was* violently extended in the direction of John's face, but only as an inoffensive member of an open-handed quintet of Duffy digits.

John was a bit taken aback by this abrupt conclusion of their interview. But, as the talk itself had been only partially informative and more than a little surreal, it was just as well. He shook Lawyer Duffy's hand. Who said, as he departed:

"My people will be in touch. Take care of yourself, son."

John imagined a troop of tiny and bushy-eyebrowed legal assistants. Duffy had no people–he enjoyed the distinction of being the sole attorney in the Plaza Tower office structure unaccompanied by partnership–but the fabrication is a common and inoffensive one. Then Duffy's farewell seemed potently soporific to John. He dozed.

*

In this sleep John saw his father. He was saying, 'Take care of yourself, son'. John was wearing a graduation gown and cap. He could not see his father in this dreamscape, but he heard the words. They were accompanied, as all things spoken by his mother and father were, by the gentle tinkling of ice cubes in a glass.

Had John's father ever given his son that directive? No. Neither father nor mother, in fact, had been present at John's high school graduation. But his father should have told him that, even in a disembodied voice. He should have known the contrary nature of his son's soul and the likely tumult it would meet with in the world at large.

The dream merged with genuine recollection, then; young John was sitting on the wrong side of the principal's desk. Graduation had yet to assemble its modestly attired chorus line of seniors that year, in John F. Kennedy High School, in Newkirk, New York. John F. Kennedy High School, formerly Franklin D. Roosevelt High School. Alexander had named a city for his horse; ideals must ever be encouraged, and freshened.

To John's left was Franks, a guidance counselor, that stately title evocative of gentle wisdom and customarily referring to a sort of hybrid social worker with a limited and pubescent clientele. All three were gathered because of an action by eighteen year-old John, an action inexplicable to the two gentlemen with him and outrageously anarchistic to one. On the principal's desk were two letters, one penned by John and one from a respected university. It was a university that had actually and rather ardently courted John's matriculation into it. John had expressed a determination to remain on the outside of the prestigious university's walls, both directly to the university and through his salivating guidance counselor. Further entreaties by the school were made, and the guidance counselor brought these to John's attention as an agent dangles a fat contract before a starving actor. All a relatively common dance, as the world enticingly crooks a finger in the face of its brightest youth. And of itself would have scarcely constituted a basis for the somewhat awful ambience in the principal's office that day.

But John's lack of interest in the distinguished school had not stopped there. Upon having been bombarded with literature extolling the traditions and brilliance of the university just one brochure too far, John had written to its office of admissions. He had written a letter which, to put it plainly, mocked its scholastic integrity, vilified its greed, excoriated its grotesque tuition structure, and—most emphatically of all—traduced what John saw as its appalling pride in supplying society with a mindless brigade of affluent zombies.

"Why did you write this, John?" The principal was not unfriendly. Merely stymied.

"Well, they wouldn't take 'no' for an answer." John was not antagonistic. Merely confident.

The guidance counselor was many things, however, and the one most apparent is hurt.

"Princeton isn't used to getting hate mail." Or, 'you insect'.

John then uttered 'I'm sorry' in the way people do when they feel they must say it as a prefix to a decidedly unapologetic response. He also slighted Franks by directing his response to the principal. "I'm sorry, but that's just too bad. I wouldn't have written a word if *they* (this with a telling glance at the enemy's accomplice, Franks) had just left me alone. But, every day, it was like there was a new packet from Princeton."

The principal, seemingly less emotionally involved with that school than Franks, tried to mollify the recruitment attempts. "John, it stands to reason that a great school would want one of our best students."

"I understand that. I just didn't want them."

Franks almost gasped. He knew the boy repudiated Princeton, but to so coldly say it, and in front of the principal…There was silence.

Then John seized what he felt might, just might, be an opportunity to explain fully.

"Sir, I don't see why they should be able to flood me with their…literature and I can't respond. I told Mr. Franks (decorum is thrown out onto the sports field, now; *j'accuse*, Franks) I didn't want to go to college. Period."

Franks, anticipating support from the right side of the desk, said: "He had to know I couldn't take that seriously."

At which point John experienced the first of what would be many definable bursts of righteous wrath within himself. "Why *not?* I said it and I meant it. Just because I do well in school doesn't mean I like it a lot."

"Princeton," whispered Franks, "is not just any school."

"Fine. Great. *I don't care.*"

Franks hissed in disbelief.

"That still doesn't explain this letter, John." The principal was sincere in his desire to understand. With heaviness of heart, John realized that that wasn't, wouldn't ever be, enough.

"It just seemed to me that they weren't happy with a plain 'no'. So I thought I should spell it out for them, once and for all. Since Mr. Franks wasn't exactly *supporting* my choice…" Franks had in fact undermined John's waiving of the Princeton invitation, by means of clandestine pooh-poohing in the ears of its admissions people.

The principal reads aloud: "…*while uninformed lectures from pitiably ignorant instructors, following nights of sleeplessness in quarters shared with pot-smoking and privileged bastards on Daddy-financed scholarships, hold a strong appeal…no single professor on your staff commands respect in any of the fields he teaches…archaic institution, more of a diploma factory for the wealthy…*" He smiled in spite of himself, the principal. He did not worship at the same altar as Franks. "This came to me, John, from a friend there. It caused…a little anxiety."

John was mute. Only a quick elevation of his eyebrows indicated regret, if regret was to be so eagerly looked for that so meager a manifestation would do.

"The fact is, it makes us look bad. And it doesn't do you any good."

Franks said, "Princeton's pretty big, you know." John sang in his mind, 'my boyfriend's back, and there's gonna be trouble…'

John then acted far in advance of his years; that is, he utterly ignored the ivy besotted and scholastically fetishistic Franks.

"Again, I'm sorry. But no, not really. I have to say again, I wouldn't have written a word if they had just left me alone."

"Well. This letter of yours, John…it seems unnecessary. A spiteful thing, really."

John heard this as intently as his school's principal wished him to. Yet he responded with these resoundingly true four words: "They asked for it." They asked for it. John, eighteen year-old John in his Levi jeans and Gap button-down shirt, knew within himself, at the moment of speaking them, that those words should be etched as a fine epitaph on someone's simple headstone. Someone decent, someone who honored the truth. He wanted that person to be himself.

"Try to remember, son, people talk to other people. People remember insults, too. And there's such a thing as cutting off your nose to spite your face."

Stitched into the air with the principal's breath, there it was. The sampler of his life, the homily that would follow and haunt John in the years to come. He didn't understand it then, either. A nose wasn't such a lot to lose. And it was somebody else's face being chastised.

As it seemed that the interview was concluded, John rose. Then he found that his left leg would not take its cue. He looked down and saw a cast on it. He turned his head, saw Franks with a grin as wide and unsettling as that of five Cheshire cats for a mercifully brief moment, and saw Rene outside the glass partition of the principal's office. She was talking to Mrs. Childress, both women were smiling, and then he woke up.

*

Day Five. John was escorted in a wheelchair to a waiting taxi. The nurses he had been tended by were on duty; one nodded and smiled as he passed, and the others were as stone. Extraordinary, thought John. Nothing of an adversarial nature had passed between himself and any of them. Yet, this coldness.

Then, as he swiveled on his heel for the backward entry into the passenger seat crutches decree, he saw Bob. His ally, the handsome outlaw. Turning into the main entrance, Bob saw John departing. He smiled broadly and gestured with his hand to his mouth, to mime the smoking of a cigarette.

In the taxi John was immeasurably delighted. There was someone who was all right, who was different. Bob. He would never see Bob again, he presumed, except perhaps during a periodic check-up. But Bob was, would always be, an exception in John's alert and guarded heart. He could be spared, when John's fictive sword went to work in John's almost daily reveries.

*

Day Five, still. Evening.

Rene was at home. Her aunt Alice Ann was out with some colleagues from her neurotically clannish Sterling Realty office. An early dinner had been prepared and consumed; what remained of her aunt's meatloaf had been preserved in plastic for a future lunch. The television was in the process of not very subliminally presenting to her the prestigious career and beautiful, albeit homosexual, male model she will attain for herself, upon the purchase and application of a certain coloring agent. The winter night outside the windows of the small house on Pickett Avenue was a frieze. Nothing, no person, no car, was moving. A frigid Pompeii in the Tennessee Valley.

She felt that night an unease, an apprehension, with which she was becoming dismally familiar.

Rene knew that John was to be released from the hospital that day. She had seen him three times during his stay and had phoned him twice. These contacts had not been unwelcome to John. Rene was aware that she was never a part of the scorn she saw him display, mildly or spasmodically furiously, at Garamond's. She knew she was exempt from his hatred; she knew he saw her differently. She knew little more than this, then.

She was thinking, just as John in his apartment was then bathing in a tub less than one third of the mass of himself he had thought perhaps he might be able to bathe, of the day of the accident. She was thinking of the ordinariness of all of it: how the police had told her of the collision; how the information that the only damage was very likely nothing more than a broken leg had come; how it had passed through the restaurant as news of any such non-fatal and not terribly interesting mishap would.

What she recalled on this night was the aloneness she had felt that day, behind the counter and around the tables. Regular patrons had made the appropriate noises and had asked the routine question such a circumstance draws forth, and Rene had supplied the facts she herself had been given. Lawyer Duffy was able to elaborate to those interested, when he came in late for his usual lunch.

But Rene had been dreadfully alone, all through it, with an incomprehension she could not share. And which was oddly absent in everyone else. The old woman had not been speeding or driving recklessly, according to the police. John was a fast, almost maniacal walker, Rene knew. She knew too that he was not one to miss things, that anything as bulky as a car would be perceived by him well before being actually seen.

Which left her on this evening of the day of John's release with the same question framed in her mind that gnawed at her on the day of the accident. It was not a question she could ask of anyone save John himself.

Why did he do it? But she knows. And wraps her arms around herself, and drops her chin into the soft valley they form.

*

As the above scene is softly played out in solitude, we take a moment to look in at a house to the east of Rene's. A young woman named Kim is in the kitchen of the first floor apartment. She is calling out to her roommate in the living room. Their dialogue is short and is exchanged in its entirety from the separate rooms.

"Did you call California?"

There is no reply. But fast thinking could be heard by anyone so aurally gifted.

"Andrea?"

"Right. I *heard* you."

There is another pause. It is under the circumstance as exasperating as it is intended to be.

"Andrea?"

"Yeah, I think I did. But I'll have to pay you next week."

At the small kitchen table, Kim counts to herself. One, two, three…

"God, you know they sent me home *twice* this week?"

Four

A Pause for Whispering

Enter, the Word. And the Word enters through many doors, and comes to many waiting ears. The locus for this particular incarnation of the Word is the multi-tiered Plaza Tower building, home to Garamond's and many other places not gastronomic in nature. As the Word likes nothing better than riding in elevators, this Word will enjoy an especially rich, if inherently brief, life.

The Word on John moves in like the 'flu, from the very hour of the accident. There are in all Words quite a few similarities to contagious infection; it is a pity that such analogies sully every Word, but this cannot be helped. For the Word is maddeningly random in whom it settles upon, just as is a virus. The girl spending hours in close contact with the sniffling colleague will play racquetball and fall healthily in love that week, while the broker's client, exposed to that same sniffler for the space of half a minute, will that evening burn, freeze and say unkind things to his wife.

So too does reasonable expectation of contagion mean very little, as far as the Word goes. If it were more predictable in its course and logical in its succession of victims, Garamond's would be quarantined, as far as something as crafty and virulent as the Word may be contained. But that would avail nothing. There is Andrea Cornell, the new server at Garamond's, hired by John despite a prickly feeling at the nape of his neck during her interview. She is young, healthy, unencumbered by a moral structure adequately complex to apportion rightness or wrongness to the wake of gossip, and a pathological liar of unimpeachable standing. She was born to carry, a Typhoid Mary of rumor. Yet she remains apart from the Word, completely. Not only does she irritatingly fail to provide the inside information customers are politely trying to extract from her, she is dully apathetic to the entire situation. Her employer got his leg busted because he purposely did not get out of the way. Even she has absorbed this much. She in fact unknowingly saw it occur. But it is nothing to her, at all. It is a lovely sunrise to an excruciating hangover. Andrea shrugs it all away, says nothing about it, and finds some scanty tips left for her in return.

Yet Rodney Bourne is all fever, and he has never even dined at Garamond's. Rodney assists, as we have seen earlier, two architects on the 20th floor. That is, he ferries on bicycle blueprints and plans between his employers and their clients, a sort of construction midwife. In this age of specialization, he is a specialized messenger boy. Blonde and so upright in appearance that one surmises in his possession the seeds of a college account begun for the children he will surely care for ten years hence, there is not one grain of gossip-mongery in his freckled being. So how to explain his fascination with the Word, with what he overheard his bosses tossing about? Hard to say. Rodney believes that he has seen John in the building, perhaps at the little post office in the center. But Rodney's virus is a mutant strain; John as John means nothing to him as yet, nor do the more pragmatic or mercenary theories of the accident's cause interest him. He inquires what he can from here and there simply because he feels that something remarkable happened. He would like, he thinks he needs, to know more. There is fine innocence and perhaps something even nobler in his curiosity. This will of course be punished, and rather soon.

Brave Rodney is one of very few contaminated with so rare a symptomatic response. The Word on John circulates freely, strongly, in the five calendar days of John's one very long day at Baptist Hospital. The candy and cigarette shop on the ground floor is dangerously loaded with germ material; customers depart from it with smokes and the newest thinking on the subject. The Word draws further strength from this itself, that new notions are taken on faith, that the person most emphatically holding forth is the person who actually knows more. When in fact no one knows anything.

There is as well a curious and nearly self-defeating aspect to the Word on John Grigio. The very thing that excites the common mind and commoner tongue about it, the impure mite isolated as the font of the strain, defies category. Even in the vast indexes of the catalogues of rumor. Once it was established, through the harmlessly intended coughing of Lawyer Duffy to a fellow attorney, that John had courted his own catastrophe, the Word evolved from the mundane recounting of a traffic mishap to something speedily premeditated and possibly juicy. The initial assumptions all around held that John Grigio made a split-second decision to clean up on an old woman's poor driving skills. Naturally. He saw the car coming, perhaps saw the diamonds on Mrs. Childress' hands glinting in the sun, and took a chance. She would strike him, he would sue, and life in Knoxville would resettle with another minor and not fully sane episode in its cluttered past of eccentric acts.

But no one buys this. It makes no sense, even to the soul most hungry for evidence of badness outside of himself. Because the greediest creature in such a circumstance could not possibly calculate beforehand the force of the impact and assess the damages to himself and those to be gleaned from the driver. And it is more fantastic, and downright frightening, to suppose that someone could be so compelled by mere greed as to invite great pain and potential crippling.

So the Word flounders. It still skips high and low, bounces off the uninterested and clings to the speculative, but not in any agreeably recognizable form. If the virus is to survive, it must mutate. Thus, by Day Three, serene nodding follows fresh analysis. Cream is stirred into coffee and order is made out of chaos. The Word is, John is unhinged. The person to first so declaim is none other than Kelly Clifton-Cass. As it is generally known that she is chummy with Rene; and as it is understood through Kelly herself that this chumminess is founded upon Rene's admiration of her; and as it is largely presumed that Rene is, if not John's sweetie, the female closest to him; and as everyone knows women exercise greater perspicacity in those arenas of life not charted by graph paper or demanding steel reinforcement; and as even men who do not truly believe in the deeper insight of womanhood will never admit to such misgivings, it is believed. John is not right, 'not right' being the Southern euphemism to blanket and billow over everything from a poor choice in clothing to cats in the freezer.

It is only fair to note that Kelly Clifton-Cass bore no ill will for John Grigio. She took no great satisfaction in branding him with a crimson 'NR'. In point of fact, very few people who take even unwittingly the responsibility for what could be the destruction of another life ever mean anything harmful by it. The angels do indeed sing, but they also weep, and have wept for ages.

And does John, upon his return to his daily life, perceive this interestingly different conception of himself? No, not at all. John is forever penetrating, gifted or cursed with that perceptiveness which makes his life in the world often miserable, and which may one day show him something splendid, unseen by all the rest. But even he can only see, now, that he receives extra glances, furtive or directly smiling. He assumes they arise from his handicapped state. Interesting. And surprisingly naïve for a true misanthrope.

Five

Rhubarb, and Rodney

It was exactly eleven weeks after the accident, and five weeks after Rene's conversation with Kelly Clifton-Cass, that the first pie from little Mrs. Childress arrived at Garamond's.

Christmas had not come to Garamond's, but it had run through and tossed a few signature items about. Sprigs of plastic mistletoe had hung above the pick-up window for one day before Rene moved them to a less trafficked aperture; cook Reggie's continual appearances through the window on that afternoon, his lips pursed in grotesque expectation, made the small redecoration a desirable thing. Two strings of lights gingerly and tentatively framed the door to the telephone and restrooms. A diminutive nativity was sandwiched on the ledge by the front door. Every patron entering inadvertently jostled the baby Jesus; His mother and the animals likewise tottered. The three kings were, as real kings have never been on this earth, stable. They had been glued to their spots.

It so happened, that afternoon, that John and Rene were quite alone behind the counter when the mail came. It was four o'clock. Club sandwiches had been the item of the day, as for no reason one particular meal will assert preeminence for an hour or two. No one can say why. No one had bit into a club sandwich early in the lunch shift and bellowed satisfaction to tables still undecided. But clubs had sprung up on table after table, like spring blooms in a patchy garden. Mayonnaise had been in the air.

Only Lawyer Duffy now occupied the café, stirring an iced tea so unceasingly and with so penetrating a gaze, that the beverage itself may well have been the subject of some groundbreaking experiment.

There were bills for Garamond's in that mail, and John scanned the envelopes of these meticulously, as though to ascertain that the sender had indeed selected the correctly indebted addressee. There was junk, too: these he tore into neat and increasingly smaller segments.

Then there was a box, a lovely and strange brown box. It was not decorated in any way. But so much care had gone into the brown cardboard folds of it, so perfectly had the almost invisible tape been applied to its edges, that the thing had the appearance of a present. As it was. Rene kept her eyes upon it throughout John's examination of his more pedestrian correspondence.

No name was printed on the package to indicate the sender. There was an address, though. And in the second it required for John to connect that address with the person to whom it must belong, Rene witnessed a shade of sadness pass over his face. As though he suspected the disappointment, the jab to misanthropy, of something kind having been sent his way from that quarter. As it had.

"Mrs. Childress." He just said the name and snaked his hands deeper into the apparatus of his crutches. He stared at the box, and one-third of his mouth attempted to shift to the corner of his left eye. That is all he did.

"Well, aren't you going to open it?" Rene had long ago tried to find ways around, and finally gave back into, stating the obvious to the man.

"I'm not sure I should."

"Why not, for heaven's sake?"

Lawyer Duffy, hearing little of this but sensing intrigue, looked up.

"It's *ex parte*."

"What?"

"*Ex parte*. I'm suing this woman, we're involved in litigation. I can't take presents from her."

"What makes you think it's a present?"

The unspoken language that can exist when even only one of two people is loved was at play, then, for John did not need to respond and Rene silently acknowledged the pointlessness of her question. Lawyer Duffy, his ears having risen a hair's breadth higher at the bandying of '*ex parte*', stirred his abused drink and listened in more intently, his focus now divided, the iced tea or the conversation behind the counter each holding possibilities.

Rene said, "Poo." She took the paring knife she used for lemons and deftly slit the edges of the box. Feeling that she had perhaps taken upon herself something litigious after all, she said, "*I'm* opening it, so there's no..."

"Culpability."

"Right. You're not..."

"Waiving any rights."

"Yes. *You're free of involvement in this action.*" So pleased was Rene by this elegant and seemingly proper pronouncement, her hands moved even more gracefully and quickly. The box lid was as neatly ready to be lifted as it had been secured by the old woman's hands. Rene removed it and there was what could be seen to be a pie inside. That is, it was a pie in a dream, for layers of wax paper gently obscured the harder edges even pies manifest in this imperfect world. And taped to the top of the uppermost layer of wax paper—taped with tiny portions of the adhesive on diagonals of the corners—was a note. It read, in the spidery and exquisite pen of two female generations past: *Hoping you enjoy this and are feeling better, Ruth.*

John and Rene peered at the thing for a moment, until Rene said, "How about that. It's a pie."

"Yeah...", John said. "A pie." And he imbued that word with such potential meaning and mysterious intent that Lawyer Duffy held his spoon still within his glass.

But Rene is of the apple-cheeked race that can do only one thing when confronted with pastry inside a box, and that is, take it out. She did so, John watching her as though she were taking a rattler by the neck.

"Now, this is strange." Rene began peeling away the wax paper.

"I'll say."

"No. I mean, this is crazy. It's still *warm.*"

John extracted a hand from the latticework of a crutch and placed his palm, gingerly, upon the pie's surface. Warm, yes. Cozily, if inexplicably, warm.

So, implacably driven by the same wholesome DNA which moved her hands to free the pie from the box' confines, Rene took up her paring knife once more and carved a tiny 'V' into the crust. This she then lifted, to expose the contents.

"What the hell is it?"

"I'm not sure." Rene brushed a fingertip across the top of the lush, purple-green filling and tasted it.

John watched her face closely. "Well? It looks like cabbage."

"John. It's not cabbage." Rene slowly smiled as awareness dawned.

"Who the hell bakes cabbage pie? Wrap it up again."

"John. It's rhubarb." A specific smile, held in reserve for the nine years since Rene had last tasted the stuff, was brought out once more on her countenance; her face was expressive of having received a friendly wave from an acquaintance nearly forgotten.

John remained thoughtful, if not downright wary. "Rhubarb. *Rhubarb.*" Then a moment from a game show, coincidentally also nine years past, came to him. "Wait. Rhubarb's poisonous. I read it some place."

Rene had never seen that particular game show, but she had had real life experience with the vegetable, albeit distant. "No, no. The *stems* are. You cook the leaves."

"Are you sure?"

"Yes. Or the leaves are, and you bake the stems. I forget. One of them will kill a dog."

"That old woman is trying to kill me."

"John."

"Again."

During this entire exchange, so halting and leery in nature, so at variance with what a pie in a box customarily engenders, it is important to note that the pie had been on the counter. Of course it had. But what is not readily felt or perceptibly taken in is that baked goods, thus displayed and intrinsically immobile, nonetheless influence the air they inhabit. This is not to say that a pie has power. But it would be equally presumptuous, and perhaps more wrong, to assert that it has none. So the mood between and around John and Rene lightened, as the dimpled and perfectly beige surface of Mrs. Childress' gift, preternaturally bumpy in every right spot, sat there.

Rene replaced a layer of paper over it. Smiling, she asked: "So you'll take it home, right?"

John, although stripped of his cynicism and mistrust concerning the article, was still John. "I don't *think so.*"

By that moment Lawyer Duffy had performed in a skeletal fashion the exercise of his talent more usually at play in his office on the 17th floor, or in the courthouse across the street. He knew of course John's recent history; all floors in the Plaza Tower did, in fact, indirectly through his having been a bystander to it. And he had observed and heard enough of the conversation between John and Rene to accurately assess what the small controversy was. He rose, walked over to the counter, placed three dollar bills upon it and said, "If you don't want it, John, I'll take it from you."

"Take it, Mr. Duffy?"

"I'll buy it. If you'll be so kind as to let me."

"You want this pie?" Something—what? Rene, you get so close, sometimes— in John's tone made Rene watch his face very carefully.

"It's been years since I had good rhubarb. No one makes it anymore."

"Ah, Mr. Duffy." John's 'ahs' were important, Rene knew. They portended refusal.

"I'm afraid I can't."

Lawyer Duffy was unruffled. John had somehow anticipated ruffling.

"No? Too bad. Well, y'all enjoy that thing, then."

Off strode Lawyer Duffy, leaving John and Rene completely alone. People walked by Garamond's like the parade of modern ghosts seen every day through its windows. Rene asked John a question, already knowing, not the answer, but what it was not.

"Why wouldn't you sell it to him? Or just let him take it?"

In wicked mimicry of Duffy, John sneeringly said, "*You-all enjoy it, now-uh.*"

"John? Why didn't you—"

"Maybe I like rhubarb."

He didn't like rhubarb. He didn't know how rhubarb tasted. That was apparent to both of them, rendering his statement the silly obfuscation it was. And he wasn't sentimental, and he had evinced no single spark of warm feeling to Mrs. Childress, as a person or as the object of his lawsuit. But he carefully and fully rewrapped the pie, returned it to its box like a parent setting an infant in his crib, and took it back to his little office.

Rene went through the motions of closing the restaurant. She wiped the clean counter again, wiped the coffee maker, and turned off most of the lights. She then reached for a bag by her handbag and removed from it a few additional ornaments, ornaments she had forgotten about with the advent of the pie. They were miniatures of characters from the 'Rudolph' animated Christmas show. She had Herbie, and Yukon Cornelius, and Charlie-in-the-box. Once, a year before, the nicest smile Rene had ever seen on John's face appeared when these characters were mentioned. She now placed the Charlie-in-the-box on the cash register's shelf. Where John would most frequently encounter it. This seemed right.

All the while, she wondered what John would do with the pie. He wouldn't let someone else have it. In fact, he was to take home, if not actually consume, all the pies the forthcoming months brought.

She called out a 'goodbye' to him, their cue that he was to lock up shortly and leave himself. And, as she removed and hung up her apron, she was suddenly sure of one thing: he was keeping the pie to himself, not out of greed, not out of his notorious spite, but as a memento of a kind she could not fathom.

*

That evening, Mrs. Ansley telephones Mrs. Childress.

"Are you all right, Ruth? Should I come by?"

"No. No, dear, I'm just fine. The truth is—"

"Because I can be there in no time at all. Ruth. I'm happy to."

"There's no *need*, Ellen. Honestly, dear. The truth is, I—"

"I should have been with you today. I do wish you'd let me, Ruth."

"It was fine, actually, dear. Everything went just as Randolph said it would."

"Independence is fine, Ruth, but we need to look after one another, don't you think, dear?"

"Have you seen their offices, Ellen? I never saw anything like it, not in a *lawyer's* office. Florals as far—"

"Did the queer boy try for more?"

"Ellen?"

"More money?"

"No. No, not at all. The truth is—"

The dialogue zigzags thusly for another two minutes, before affectionate goodbyes are said and receivers are delicately returned to their cradles. And what the truth is, or what at least it was to Ruth Childress that day, goes unspoken.

*

One of the things that sets Rodney Bourne apart from the majority of other men in their early twenties is that time is for him realistically paced. If he is dating a girl for a few months, then he is dating a girl for only a few months, and he does not feel it or mark it as an especially lengthy period. As young people will. A year hence is not a lifetime away, but a year, and he has observed that everything will arrive or fail to come by somebody's clock, if not his own. This is not to suggest that he is a sloppy messenger for Titch and Pratt, Architects and Surveyors; rather, his equanimity embraces the larger prospects, for good and ill, the rest of the world impatiently watches for signs of boiling.

So it is in the last week December of 1996 that he pedals his Schwinn back from an errand. It is the final mission of his day, and Titch and Pratt were farewelled by him before he set out. Yet here he is again in the parking deck of the Plaza Tower, chaining his bicycle to the post he always uses.

As cars store heat, parking lots hoard cold. The winter air seems to greedily coalesce with the trapped fumes of the garage, gaining through it ballast, more permanent residency and, in air circles, a greater market share. It is nearly tactile, the cold. Rodney pockets the key to the padlock and pulls his sheepskin coat closer about him. His freckles sting his ruddy face.

The army of moderately skilled office labor currently strewn throughout the Tower is still in residence; it is early in the afternoon, just past one. Rodney has no strict plan for what he has chosen to do this hour. But he has an honest and humane ambition. Far better than a plan, such a motive is, and usually far less efficacious.

He steps to the elevator, knowing only that he will go to Garamond's and order a hot chocolate. That is the extent of his actual scheme. The body, or heart, of it lies in a hope that perhaps accidentally, either through seeing John Grigio or hearing anything at all, he will begin to understand what has been on his mind for the past three months. He has by no means obsessed over the mystery, mostly abandoned by the Plaza Tower hive for quite some time, of John's accident. But he wished to know more, from the day he first caught a few notes of the gossip in barbershop quartet style

in the Plaza lobby. He does not, as has been stated, know John. Nor is
Rodney Bourne a hero. Yet he has from the start detected a calumny he
does not care for set upon the person of John, and we would need no
heroes at all if every man exercised the minimal stretch of imagination
required to envision himself as the center of unsubstantiated defamation.
So he wants to know more. As no more has in any way presented itself to
him, he will go after what he can.

That the simplicity of his ambition is as cliched as the tuft of blonde
hair on his Saxon brow, that the good impulse guiding him is as ridiculously hackneyed as each single freckle on his face, may be true. But is only
mildly funny to the unfreckled and ignoble.

*

Rodney steps into the coffee-scented warmth of Garamond's and takes
a seat at the small counter. Andrea, who is just then untying her apron
strings as her standard, yet always denied, signal that she will be clearing
out as soon as Rene caves in, stops her fingers in their very unlooping.
Looping in fact is re-engaged, as is her best and most unassuming smile.
She slips on the face in her repertoire most natural.

"Hello there. Need a menu?" So might a lioness inquire if an antelope
cared for a stroll deeper into the jungle.

"Thanks, no. Just a hot chocolate." He smiles in return, a genuine version of the miserably false display facing him. As a reward he is quickly
treated, not to the cocoa he desires, but to something less sweet and more
cloying: Andrea, now *coy*.

For Andrea has seen this boy before. She noticed him on the day she
first presented herself to John and Garamond's as a little dynamo, a serving wonder waiting to be unleashed, months before; they had passed one
another in the building's lobby. She saw him again at the end of October,
in Garamond's itself. He had come in, Rene had greeted him before she
could fly out from behind the counter–thus establishing Rene as a slut, as

well as a domineering cow, in the circuitry of Andrea–and she, Andrea, had quite literally stamped her little feet in impotent rage. For the remaining twenty minutes of Rodney's sojourn, Andrea had bombarded him with flashes of teeth from strategic points around the café. This in turn had prompted Rodney to innocently ask of Rene who the smiling girl was. Which was then misinterpreted by Rene as a potentially frightening and altogether lamentable expression of interest in her colleague. Not surprisingly, Andrea had sensed the brief exchange of question and answer from a distance as pertaining to her. She had been gratified on several levels, none of them human.

"You *sure*? Just hot chocolate, now?" She even hikes one shoulder up, leaning against the counter to issue the question. She attempts to fuse innocence with brass; it is her ultimate alchemic ambition, as wizards once bought time from gullible princes with promises of securing gold from lead. In Andrea's young life, in the dependably crooked paths she has already taken, there have been many courts, and many princes left with a surplus of lead, powerless anger, depleted treasuries and no gold at all.

"Yeah, thanks. Just hot chocolate." Rodney even nods, to doubly confirm what is apparently a peculiar request to the girl. He perceives nothing but an uncommon reaction to an ordinary order. That is the thing about real goodness. It has no nose for duplicity of any kind and stumbles through the dark of it, bruising itself. Antelopes are luckier, blessed with both speed and an inbred antipathy towards lionesses.

Andrea raises her thin eyebrows in an even less explicable way. It is an expression of reluctant acceptance of a request, hinting at knowledge of unvoiced desires from the individual making it. It brings forth no response from Rodney, as it engendered no reaction of any kind within him. Andrea turns her back to prepare the drink and decides, in no particular order, to become romantically involved with this boy, and to hurt him.

She sets the hot chocolate on the counter, away from his reach. Coyness is oddly resilient for something so eel-like; she says, as to a child, "Bet you'd like some whipped cream on this?"

Rodney—if this were a movie house, a hundred voices would cry out, Run!—bats not one blonde lash, nor shifts one freckle. "Doesn't matter," he replies. The words are spoken pleasantly enough. Andrea's brand-new design hardens. The romance will be the more intense, and the hurting of a crippling variety.

Six

Demonstrating Sibling Affection

As the above encounter proceeds, another, more caring, yet identical in its participants' gargantuan ignorance of each other's aims, takes place halfway in Lawyer Duffy's simple offices. Halfway, because the intercourse in which he shares is telephonic. He is calling his sister, to ascertain her impression of the gentleman she had seen the evening before.

Duffy's practice is dependent upon Duffy alone for its life. He has no partners. There is Duffy, and there is nothing else but more Duffy. More for form's sake than to answer any real need, a clerk assists him three days out of the week, in filing and neatening and occasionally looking up. Thus his office becomes, as the offices of lone men frequently do, a bachelor in itself. It is dry, devoid of ornamentation; diehard bachelors are not in the habit of primping, there being no need. It is a little wide in the middle, between foyer and *sanctum sanctorum* in the rear, just where men with no loving constraints on their dietary excesses expand in the fullness of time. And it bore no perceptible character, this office, save that of an irrefutable thereness. When we pause to reflect upon the single men of middle years in our acquaintance, we walk around and around that very thereness, looking for more and coming back to only more of the same.

"Lou?" His feet are resting upon an ottoman in his inner chamber, his cigar unlit and fat between his fingers. He will not light it until he feels confident in a conversation of duration enough to warrant the indulgence.

"Yes, Randolph." In her apartment, Louisa Duffy tightens. She was expecting the call, as she awaits fond interrogation following every evening arranged by her brother. She removes her reading eyeglasses, though, and in that manner those who wear them do when it is time to get down to business.

"How are you today, dear?"

"I am well, Randolph." It is only in these circumstances, only when Lawyer Duffy tries to extract from his sister news of romantic hope born from his devoted machinations, that his sister is, not rude, but cold to him. Ordinarily she is the stereotypically adoring little sister to his senior brotherhood, as they have been to one another for over fifty years. She is aware of the chill in her voice now, hears it in her own tone, regrets it, but cannot help it. When Duffy interrogates his sister after dates, he is to her a different man, as wives view husbands changed by drink. And Louisa Duffy makes the swift transitions to her persona that such wives almost instantaneously make.

"Did you have a good time last night, Lou? With Daniel?"

Daniel. Louisa has lately proposed to herself the theory that her brother is no longer content to passively watch for potential brothers-in-law; that, as the years pass and her innocence remains unassaulted, he has taken a more active and, if so, utterly unacceptable role of coercion, by means of the legal sway he wields in town. Oh, God, she has thought. Oh, God, no.

Daniel, for the record, is the name she recalls from last night. But it is a faceless name. There was a lot of beige, either on him or within him, perhaps a mustache, a definite career in insurance, but no face at all. She knows too that they dined, because she feels uneasily redolent of herbs today and because she remembers playing with a basket of bread for two hours.

"It was fine, Randolph." As she speaks, her eye is drawn again and again to the small advertisement in the magazine she had been reading. In it a robust and shirtless young man is standing with his hands held up in an attitude of careless abandonment. The photograph is meant to promote a variety of shaving cream. Or a car. Strangely, and contrary to the task for which he is being paid, the young man is pictorially informing Louisa Duffy that it's time, and there isn't a lot to spare.

"Did you like him at all, Lou? Would you say you hit it off?"

At this stage in her life, Louisa Duffy no longer even entertains the idea of hitting it off as desirable, let alone possible. She does not want to hit it off, if ever she did. She sees her face in the mirror above the telephone table in her apartment's pretty living room, a helmet of gray waves framing a square of large, perfectly even, features. There is not even a trace of asymmetry, to render the face more interesting. It is the face she has always had and always will, unpromising, dully masculine in the utilitarian aspect of the nose and mouth and eyes, and lately creased with the folds of age. And behind this face today, as on every day since girlhood first bloomed within Louisa Duffy, she desires to briefly be with a beautiful young man. Stupid is fine. Unkind is of no consequence. Hot, now as then, is everything she wishes for.

When she was young herself the ambition was perhaps more evocative of pathos. As she ages, interestingly, it becomes more so, and not at all ridiculous. For this lust within her might only be sadly humorous if it were indulged, and indulged on a regular basis. But there has never been a beautiful young man in her arms, not even for an hour. The factors of: her brother's ceaseless protection, for as long as she can remember; his and her own status in the town, and the unthinkable reaction to her somehow, even fleetingly, securing for herself the unthinkable passion; and a modicum of cowardice that has drawn her back from the very few situations wherein her dream of physical union with a mindless and breathtaking boy might have been achieved, all combine, still, to leave her as she is. Plain, not actually unhappy, stricken with internal fits of unconsummated longing, and doomed to sit in restaurants with the beige men her brother thinks suitable for her.

"He was all right, Randolph. I'm not sure I could say we'll be seeing one another again, though." This, she has learned, is the best way to convey to Lawyer Duffy the outrageousness of even suggesting that either she or the bland fool with whom she was trapped would ever, in a million years, consider contacting the other.

"Well. That's just too bad, Lou. He's a fine man, you know."

As if she were a vixen who had toyed with the heart of the man. Louisa Duffy does not rue her lack of beauty, generally speaking; but when such other worldly imputations are made, however innocently, she wishes for it. It is not her face that has been her downfall, she believes, but her life, built around it for her and without her cooperation. As it has never been love she has sought, but the infamous thrills her life will never permit.

Ah, well. There will be others, her brother assures her. Thus does a surgeon encouragingly wave to point out a cabinet brimming with razors and knives. He is disheartened by her unenthusiastic recounting of her date, but he is still a Duffy. Steadfastness is emblazoned on the Duffy crest in the form of a plow.

Miss Duffy returns the receiver to its cradle and does not so much think about her brother's words, as she automatically falls into the reverie triggered by every such call made after every such lifeless evening. It is then that her large and ungainly eyes spark, and the small smile shaped by her too rectangular mouth becomes slyly pleased. She thinks she will hire a male escort. She thinks, as she has many times before, that money is not an issue, and that all she need do is guarantee that the rendezvous be absolutely clandestine.

She is not at these moments pretty, but she is oddly attractive.

SEVEN

OF AN AMBULATORY NATURE, WITH DR. PERKEY PROMINENT

The waiting room of Dr. Ring Perkey is an upholstered purgatory. Twenty-four chairs in a chemically gestated variation of green satin with cream piping are there, always and forever, their backs wearily against the walls or more anti-socially against one another. They mutely take their turns, like gum-chewing dance hall girls, in temporarily accommodating unhappy, or broken, visitors.

It is perhaps more reasonable to wonder what chairs might say if speech were in their power, rather than to conjecture upon the musings of walls. Walls are flat and unpromising; gifted with articulation, what could they offer not flat, not one-dimensional? Chairs have breadth. What is more, chairs have legs. Like we do. We should be able to expect good things from that quarter, when we turn for insight to the inanimate.

But these chairs, like the disreputable ladies they bring to mind, are immune to feeling. There can be no tenderness in them. Too many fists have been impatiently pounded into their seat cushions; too many cheeks have shifted in irritation and anger. Dr. Perkey's chairs have indeed heard it all. But they would not speak if they could, there being no point in doing so.

At three-forty in the afternoon of January 21, 1997, John Grigio sat in this room.

January has long since done its business in inaugurating with much fanfare almost precisely what preceded it. As months go, sadly, it has little to offer once the ribbon-cutting is done, and stays with us for thirty long days like a comedian who opens with his best joke and has nowhere else to go.

Dr. Perkey occupies a suite in Baptist Hospital, just a stroll across the bridge from the Plaza Tower building and where, through the windows of his waiting room, all of Knoxville could be seen like a nervous boyfriend outside in the cold. To John's right CNN spewed forth names and actions at that hour most prominent in the public's mind, or at least most prominent in the minds of those employed by CNN.

Three-forty. John was due to see Dr. Perkey at three. In five minutes, when he makes his pained way to ask one of the giggling women behind the receptionist's counter just how much longer, exactly, he need wait, he will be told that his doctor has been unexpectedly detained. Someone shot a bullet into the leg of a man waiting for a bus on Gay Street, just half an hour before. The receptionist so explaining will have stopped giggling with her colleagues to make this same announcement repeatedly, to others equally perturbed by the delay in their appointments, throughout the remainder of the afternoon. She will receive for her trouble a variety of responses, but all will reflect one degree or another of surprise and sadness and, best of all, guilt. Tongues will cluck on both sides of the sliding glass. It is not often that the receptionist has at her disposal so potent an excuse to offer restless patients. She does not silently wish for more such acts of random violence, but she is human; there is a minute twinkle of satisfaction in her eye as she calls upon this sad tale, again and again.

John will say, "Well. I'm still waiting." Under his breath, a moment and a step away later: "Jesus Christ."

So John sat, and waited. Waiting as such was not an especially disagreeable thing to him. He was usually able to occupy his thoughts in idle ways, to allow his mind to pursue avenues industrious or wasteful; a kind of knitting, without the yarn. It was powerlessness that vexed him. It was waiting when the termination of it rested completely in someone else's cavalier hands.

Resting across his lap and jutting above the cream piping of the arm of his chair is his walking stick. It is new. That is to say, it is very old, but only recently given to him. It came in the mail two days before. From Mrs. Childress.

The stick is extraordinary. It is of a heavily lacquered and gnarled wood, the variety of which John is unsure. When the lengthy and tubular package arrived at his home, John knew the sender, not by the return address, but by the careful taping of it. There may have been a scent, too, but that is a possibility he leaves alone.

He sat and recalled his reaction upon first being handed the box. He had thought, it must be a gun. He did not think this in a way indicating a vicious intent from Mrs. Childress; he did not imagine her wishing to see him dead. John did, however, see in his mind a thought like a moth, only there for a moment, in a corner, and then gone: she sent a gun that he might end his own misery.

As with the pies–rhubarb, apple and coconut had so far been prepared by and sent from the no doubt cozy kitchen of Ruth Childress, with pecan in the wings–there was hesitation on John's part as to the proper reaction. That is, there had been hesitation with rhubarb, a faster acceptance of apple (and an odd little greed, too, born with the coming of that apple pie), and coconut custard had been taken in as an old friend, albeit guiltily. But the change in manner of gift with the advent of the walking stick reawakened the rhubarb wariness. A parade of pies was one thing; each had paved the way for the easier reception of the next. But the cane was something else. Inedible, it would always be there, if accepted. John had telephoned his lawyers. Gilley, French and Sweet.

Gilley had been of course unavailable since 1988. French was too important to be in and Sweet had migraine. John had then briefly informed Miss Marchbanks, secretary to all three—Gilley's demise having only minimally lessened his correspondence—of what he had been given. He did not ask Miss Marchbanks what to do about it. He assumed she would bring the matter before one of the two great men of the office.

"I'll tell Mr. Sweet, Mr. Gree-gee-o. But I can tell you right now, he'll say, use the stick." There was a pause. "That's what *I'd* say, for sure." Another pause, during which John considered, and not for the first time, the woman's arcane career with the law firm. Then she added: "Wasn't that *sweet?*"

For a moment John had been unsure if this last exclamation from Miss Marchbanks was a question actually directed to him in regard to the Childress present, or one posed to an office occupant and predicated by a possible sighting of the firm's second partner. So he let silence take over and provide, through its continuance, the answer.

"Oh. Yes. Sweet. Well, thank you, Miss Marchbanks." The telephone receiver was halfway to its cradle when John heard from it, faintly, "And eating them pies! 'Bye, now."

A door opened from the side of the reception counter and a young man with a shock of yellow and pink hair atop his head called out, "Mr. Householder." John's brow furrowed, suddenly and uncomfortably unsure if patients were given preferential treatment through mortgage assessments, when Mr. Householder himself, asleep four chairs away, was jabbed in the ribs by what looked to be Mrs. Householder.

Sixteen pairs of eyes watched Mr. Householder make his way to the beckoning door, make his way with no cast and no limp and no visible disability at all. Ten of those eyes didn't at all care for Mr. Householder just then, and two—John's—despised him and his strong walk. The door closed, sealing Mr. Householder off in the coveted wing wherein actual treatment is done. John turned his eyes and his hatred to the CNN's female anchor. Clearly a streetwalker with connections, he surmised.

Three-fifty. A smiling man emerged from the privileged regions wherein Doctor Perkey works his plaster magic, a beaming woman rose from her green *faux* satin perch to greet him, and they left the premises as gleefully as newlyweds. Hatred was now pumping healthily in John's heart. In fairness to him, weaker cousins of that emotion could be detected within the breasts of several others present.

Then, at five minutes past four, the young man with the confectioner's hair once more opened the door he guarded. Clipboard in hand, he paused and made eight hearts beat like those of schoolgirls. In that very pause, John had turned his head down; superstitiously, he reasoned that by not looking, he would be the one sought. But he was suddenly stunned. The walking stick, on his lap still, its head protruding from between the chair's arm and his own thigh, had a face carved into it. How can he not have noticed that before? In that second he was frightened, although not by a perceived sense of malice from Mrs. Childress. By something, but not by that.

"John...Greye-gee-o?" The boy, evidently of the Marchbanks school of pronunciation, pronounced his name with all the g's hard and added the creative twist of lengthening the first vowel. Disdain surfaced on John's personable countenance and quelled the momentary unease brought on by the face on the stick. He slipped the cane from its resting posture, slapped his hand over the image etched into it, and brokenly strode to where answers and relief awaited. Maybe.

*

The relief to be had for him was provided only barely, and by answers far from satisfactory. But, in this our world, the visit to the doctor that supplies more is the exception, be you well or ill, recluse or extrovert.

First the x-rays had been taken. As in some disturbingly specific form of pornography, the ancient female technician had fumbled with John's trousers, assisting him when no help was required and then disappearing into the darkroom when a little aid would have been welcome. Then he had been relegated to one of what appeared to be dozens of baby waiting rooms, each with a charming color code and the musty, thick air of a place not ever liked. Then, ten minutes later, entered Dr. Ring Perkey. He carried in his hand x-rays and wielded them like treaties he was not confident of getting the enemy to sign.

"John. This has been, I tell you, one hell of a day."

Dr. Perkey is bright and cheerful. Everybody knows he is bright and cheerful, and no one ever invokes his last name as the quite fitting adjective it is for the man. Some things are so obvious as to be embarrassing.

"I heard about the gunshot," John said. No matter his bitterness, he behaves in the expected ways–usually–and makes the requisite remarks.

"Wasn't that something?" said Perkey, and John wondered how many times he has made or will make this startling observation that afternoon. Along with whatever John knew was coming.

Perkey fastened the x-rays to clips over fluorescent lights, like fine lingerie on a backyard line. His back to John, this is what was coming: "Makes you think, what kind of a world are we living in. A man waits for a bus and gets shot." More awfully, he turned to face John as he asked, and not rhetorically, "Is the whole world crazy?"

John's eyebrows rose as far as the muscles in his face permitted, by way of response. He shook his head in silent communion over rampant madness. In point of fact he was at that moment more concerned with what was going on in his left knee, and just a little and freshly dubious of his doctor's intellectual capacity. John did not welcome, in the midst of his disquieting ignorance over his own ambulatory condition, that the medical officer in charge of it was given to such bland commentary. We do not associate sharp minds with small talk.

Then Perkey nimbly shifted to the business at hand.

"How are you getting along? Not too well?"

With alarm at those last three words and the sudden sensibility that his doctor sought to corroborate forthcoming bad news with testimony from the patient, John said, "No." Perkey nodded his head in a sad and sage fashion. This did not help.

John amplified: "I can get around. But I don't know how much of that is because it's getting better, or because I'm used to it. It doesn't *feel* like anything's improving. There."

The 'there' was not of the 'so there!' variety, but a redundant reference to the area of injury.

Perkey may as well have scripted John's response, so dismally wise was his nod then. "Well. The good news is, the break is doing fine." He gestured to a portion of the x-ray, wherein cloudy and beautiful whiteness made an orthopedic halo around the bone fracture. "You made a lot of sticky stuff. That's looking just fine."

'Sticky stuff'. Sticky stuff. This was the fourth time John had heard that term employed, by either Dr. Perkey or a technician. It was, not to put too fine a point to it, poisonous to him. Maybe, he mused in the space of a second, the villain who had that very day pumped a bullet into a man waiting for a bus had just himself left a doctor's office, having heard 'sticky stuff' one time too many. Did the good doctor think that, had they used whatever the correct terminology was, John would be unable to comprehend the matter to which they were referring? Had he mistakenly stumbled into pediatrics for treatment?

Impatience suddenly gained control of John's soul. This is a quality never content to remain unexpressed, in John or in nice, normal people; thus it was manifested clearly on his face and in his voice, and came through as a sharply business-like focus and tone: "What's going on with the knee, then? That's where the pain still is, so I'm assuming that's where you're seeing the problems."

"Yes."

"And you're seeing…?"

"Tearing. That is, John, the tearing is worse than I thought."

A pause ensued. John was in no hurry to end it and sensed that Perkey was in the habit of allowing the patient to draw the conclusion. In his own time. And in this pause John reflected on all that he had done. Not only in courting his crippled state, but everything; as those people inches away from death are said to be granted the dubious gift of seeing their whole lives flash before them. He saw thousands of innocent contrivances engineered by himself, the best of them tiny kindnesses to others, the worst of them harmless maneuvers for his own benefit, or to teach a lesson destined to go unheeded. He saw more recent fits of rage within himself brought on by what the world saw as ordinary activity and common human behavior, fits of rage expressed by a closed fist slamming against a wall. He saw interludes of himself at home, quite alone, quite happy, and still just a little resentful. Then he saw the opposite corner of Clinch Street, the Rubicon he crossed by not crossing, and the face of Mrs. Childress through her windshield, not seeing him.

"So…you *will* have to operate."

Grateful for the quickness of John's assessment and the stoic calmness with which it had been delivered, Perkey smiled broadly and not altogether appropriately. "Yes. We have to go in." Field Marshall Perkey, valiantly smiling at a troop of one.

Don't be so goddamn happy about it, thought John. For Christ's sake, you were near tears earlier over some clown at a bus stop, thought John.

"I understand," said John. The troop would rather not go in, and would most definitely have liked more confidence behind the Field Marshall's smile.

Perkey elaborated somewhat. "The trouble with knees is the car-ti-lage." This last uttered by Perkey as to a stranger to the English tongue. "Cartilage isn't bone."

"Right," said John. "I do know that, Doctor." This was grossly unfair. The spite of his action merited a broken bone. It did? All right, it did. But months, many more months, of complications? Of apparatus and visits to this place, of waiting rooms smugly unwilling to indulge a patient's need for a smoke when nervous smoking is most called for?

"When it's torn, we can hope for a natural healing, but even the smallest tear can mean surgery."

"Right," said John. Suddenly a horrid precognition dawned within him, and it didn't bear upon pending surgery or ripped knees. He stood, to signal a need to end the interview and schedule the next visit. To get out, fast.

"Cartilage," said Dr. Perkey, "doesn't make sticky stuff."

FURTHER EVIDENCE OF FAMILIAL ATTENTIONS; MISS DUFFY AT THE LIBRARY

Alice Ann Dacres is the aunt of Rene; she is her late father's sister. She is voluptuous.

In late middle-age, she is reminiscent of a peach which has dodged plucking and eluded teeth all the way to late August. This captures the attention of strangers, and then the attention is held by something more. Namely, that there is not one single thing about her not suggestive of waiting. Anticipation is in her eyes, which began life at normal size but grew, as the necks of giraffes, to meet a need. She speaks quickly, always prepared to be cut off mid-sentence, and in hasty breaths. And her frame, yet worthy of favorable comparison to an hourglass in her fifty-fifth year, is forever set, standing or sitting, on a forward incline. Silent speculation has gone on in the minds of various Dacres' and others as to how, exactly, the woman sleeps. No one knows; Alice Ann is a maiden aunt. If she has been tenderly watched in repose, her partners have been gentlemanly and kept silent. But the smart money adds an imaginary pillow as a prop under her back.

What is Alice Ann waiting for? What is most anyone waiting for?

On the last day of January in 1997, her expansive and darting eyes are, now and then, fixing for brief seconds on the television. She and Rene have had their dinner and are settled in the living room for the evening. The two women share the pristine and petite house on Pickett Avenue left to Rene after her father's demise. Alice Ann contributes to their shared existence cleanliness of a high order; pleasant, if restless, company; and a biweekly stipend from a job she absolutely adores and has adored for the past twelve years. She is the well-liked office manager for a crew of realtors so demonstratively affectionate to one another, they might very well be a sports team.

The news is on the television. It is a local program, so there are as well continual blasts of color and sound to testify to the station's concern for its viewers and its deftness in keeping them abreast of what they already know.

Rene has a magazine on her lap, a fashionable periodical from a larger city. She is looking at a dress she does not understand, and examines it like a blueprint for something thermonuclear.

"Maybe," Alice Ann says, as though cued to do so by an unseen presence on the stair, "I should give Carolyn a call."

Rene makes an encouraging sound by way of reply, her gaze still on the mystifying frock.

"Although it's her turn."

"Oh, call. I'm sure she'd love to hear from you."

"Well, of *course*," Alice Ann confirms, to make it true. "I know she'd like to *hear* from me, for goodness' sake." Let the record reflect that, despite the almost unnatural levels of friendliness extant within the confines of Sterling Realty Associates, Carolyn does not much care for Alice Ann. If it is indeed her turn to call Alice Ann, the rotation is based only upon one previous such call made by Carolyn, and that to clarify some appointment confusion for the following day. The two are not enemies, but they are adamantly not friends. Everyone at Sterling knows it, no one talks about it, and no one understands it. For these very reasons and for none other, Carolyn does not attempt to warm to Alice Ann; the removal of the slight tension between them would simply disturb too much. For those reasons, and for the additional one of Carolyn's obstinacy, Alice Ann woos her friendship.

Rene turns the page. The dress is to her simple heart a Dead Sea scroll, and best left to scholars in these things. Photographs of intensely alive celebrities at a club no one has yet heard of, but which will be roped off to the general populace before the next issue of that magazine hits the stands, now confront her. Somehow, this brings John to her mind.

Just then, her aunt says, "And how's your friend at work?"

"Fine." Casually asked, flatly answered. As always.

"And how's his *leg*?" This, as though in reference to a near relation of John's.

Rene looks up, not dreamily, but with a cluster of thoughts in evidence on her brow.

"Well. It's not really very good." She is in the habit of supplying only barely minimal information to her aunt regarding John. Alice Ann disapproves of the affection within her niece for John Grigio, as Rene knows full well. But Rene's caring is not a flimsy thing; it won't allow itself to be cloaked under the present circumstance of his disability, and certainly for nothing as trivial as a womanly duel of sorts.

"Oh, my." Flatter than Rene's 'fine', yet directed to a ghost above the front door. "Bones, you know," she continues, "get harder with age. I mean, Ren, they don't heal so fast."

"John is only thirty-four, Alice Ann."

This fact is swiftly stored by Alice Ann in a way not at all osteopathic. That is, her femaleness notes one thing: her niece knows the man's age, exactly. Oh, my.

"That doesn't matter, sweetie. Age is age."

Rene's eyebrows arch in reluctant acceptance of this valid, if immaterial, statement.

"Anyway. It isn't the broken bone that's the problem. It's his knee."

Alice Ann tucks her shapely legs beneath her, on the small sofa. She demurely fingers the edge of her housedress. These are the long-established and nearly required tics of a woman long-established, to the world and to herself, as fetching. Alice Ann never married, but not for lack of suitors.

"Do they know what's wrong, dear?"

"His knee..." Rene begins. Then she shrugs. Everybody knows about knees.

As though possessed, the volume on the television explodes to promote a lewd video game geared for teenagers. Sex spills onto the carpet for sixty seconds.

"Oh, that's just awful. He's in for it now." To give credit where it is due, Alice Ann does not utter this with any trace of glee. The fact is, she does not *care for* John Grigio. She has met him only once, during which exchange at Garamond's he was friendly and polite. She knows as well that her niece has feelings for him, albeit of a peculiar and hazy kind. She loves her niece and wants happiness for her. But she does not *care for* John Grigio.

Love emboldens her now, as it has in the past. "He lives alone, isn't that right, honey?"

"Yes."

There is a pause. In it Rene comes to a decision. At Garamond's, that John had no visible relationship of any kind excited little or no comment. Even a Knoxvillian restaurant is imbued with the world-weariness of its five-star cousins in chic locales; intimate details carry the lasting power of today's headlines in such places. But perhaps all the innuendo she has heard at the restaurant regarding John's accident, the less ordinary and non-romantic head-shaking she has had to witness over that, renders her aunt's periodic speculations as to John's private life, just now, a form of innuendo she cannot let go by.

"Makes you wonder," Alice Ann says. Which always indicates unassailable certainty on the part of the speaker of the phrase.

"About?"

"Hm?" Alice Ann's eyes dart from the wall to the sideboard to her niece's face.

"I said, he lives alone. You said, makes you wonder. So I asked, wonder about what?"

At this Alice Ann's eyes are fixed and, for her, for a very long time. She is thrown. The sequence just recounted by Rene is of a clarity and precision she, Alice Ann, does not often encounter at Sterling Realty. Seconds pass in silence. The air in the room has thickened, a scentless and palpable miasma.

"Well, honey. Rene..." Alice Ann's gaze struggles for its accustomed and frenzied freedom, but in vain. Then inspiration seizes her and the eyes fly once more. "I'll just say this. I never knew an attractive man—*in his thirties*—who wasn't married for a reason." In triumph, she smoothes the hem of her housedress.

Rene has a generous soul. Suddenly she feels that she is asking too much of her aunt, that the confrontation so at the ready isn't worth the discomfort it has already drawn forth in Alice Ann. Who does indeed love her niece, who in turn fully knows it. Rene believes inarticulately that a foundation of real love is demeaned by the silly demands of an insistence upon a mutually preferred wallpaper. This is the wisdom to save the world, if the world would only now and then test the firmness of what's under its feet before doing anything else.

So she smiles, sweetly, with her lips pursed, and says, "Aunt *Aaaa*-lice. As beautiful as you are, *you* never married." There is just enough teasing in this otherwise potentially overbroad flattery to make the equation exactly right. The air is thinned and freshened.

The rest of the evening passes in calm. Alice Ann looks for no opportunity to mention, as she has once and calamitously before, her opinion that John is homosexual. She believes this, of course. A minor motivation in her wooing of the friendship of the inflexible Carolyn is that she wants to tell her that John is homosexual, as homosexuality is just the sort of topic the two most suave women at Sterling Realty should discuss. But, soothed by her niece's grace or disinclined to challenge in Rene what is ultimately better than in herself, she chooses to think: she's not a stupid girl, thank God. She wouldn't lose her head over a gay man.

It is worth noting here that Alice Ann's busy eyes would possibly flit at hitherto unrecorded speeds, had she been able to truly read her niece's heart. And seen that, not only did Rene disbelieve in Alice Ann's assessment of John's intimate life, she was uninterested in it. And for a reason her aunt would never, ever understand.

*

One day later. Here is Louisa Duffy again, now at the library.

The loneliness inherent in the body of a library is removed from its more woeful cousins. Most who enter enter alone, as happens in cocktail bars; and all who leave exit alone, as should happen in cocktail bars. But even human beings least able to confront isolated hours in their existences are just fine, in the library. No one is watching to gauge success, or popularity. The clientele of the library is above social reproach or pity. They need nothing save what the shelves offer. It is ironic that the hanging of a spinning and mirrored ball above the computer island would highlight them all with the attractiveness some wish they could present in other arenas.

But this is February, and the Knoxville winter is slow to sense how very unwelcome it has become. Knoxville doesn't get it; it has murmured disapprovingly, yawned theatrically, and looked at its watch with vast import. Yet winter hangs on, heedless, rude, Yankee-like. The Lawson McGhee library downtown is then sought more as a source of warmth than as the stunted citadel of enlightenment it is taken to be in temperate months. Citizens in winter, by no means of the homeless tribe, linger over books longer than they would in, say, June. Students in particular, as oil is costly and not all parents are unceasingly bountiful. But, what of it? Books are uncanny things and must be, if not read, walked by, or their contents eeriely change. If heat and not erudition brings in the frostbitten, heap high the coal, Lawson, and fan the fire, McGhee.

Miss Duffy is the most senior of those who volunteer their time to the institution. She is not precisely legendary, as the building's relatively modest age precludes such a status, but she is a well-known figure to all who see her there. Which is, sadly, not everybody who goes there. The leaden hue of Miss Duffy's helmet of hair, the extraordinarily bland aspect to her square face and only more blurrily defined squareness of form, fuse to present the world with a figure it does not always take in. And, in the fustiness of even a modern library, her being is further dulled, like a porcelain cameo on a plate of bone china.

Miss Duffy is whistling, and handling newspapers obsolescent twenty years previously. It is early evening, and she likes the early evenings best. The dark adds sexy nuance to what passes through her when attractive college boys pass by her. She now stops what she is doing, scans the first floor with a practiced and not purely lecherous eye, and looks to the wall. The thin, long windows opening onto Walnut Street reveal only patches of dirty snow, ignorantly stubborn remnants of last week's storm, clinging here and there on the curb. Across the street is the nearly Dickensian sight of a small and very old lawyer's office. Miss Duffy then realizes that, in all these years, she has never once witnessed anyone either enter or exit that building.

The day and the scene is admittedly grim. But Louisa Duffy is not. Noting the continuously untrespassed state of the invisible lawyer's humble edifice is disheartening, but only momentarily. Besides, she has had good reason over time to become inured to the bleakness, the dryness, within and without all things legal.

So Louisa goes about her business in an inoffensively brisk way. She picks up the tune she'd been whistling, softly. She notes in the paper she holds that things are looking rather bad for President Nixon, and she recognizes once more how agreeable this volunteer work is to her. One good thing about library employment of her rank is that it is self-perpetuating. People never replace books correctly, they never understand the elementarily alphabetical signs on the ends of the aisles denoting the authors contained therein, and they even, quite often, have no idea whatsoever of why they came in. For a book, yes. But their goal, many a time, stops there. So Louisa Duffy tidies up their carelessness, deciphers the signs, and advises on selection. She is good at all these things.

Just now, in fact, at six-thirty on this February evening, Miss Duffy's talents are called upon. A woman of similar years to her is floundering within the cabinetry of the very newspaper files she is re-sorting. Louisa speedily goes to her rescue, and very nearly accomplishes it. Except that, as the two circle around the specific time frame the visitor needs to journalistically isolate, Miss Duffy notices a young man at the computer island in the center of the first floor. Another good thing about libraries, and the reason they make for such wonderful settings for intrigue in film, is the labyrinthine quality to the floor plans. A person may easily conjure the pretext of an urgent duty and vanish, the fictional task and its consummation then a matter of blind faith. Miss Duffy has accumulated a roster of approximately a dozen such imaginary emergencies of an archival nature. She employs number seven now, and tells the still slightly confused patroness that she must relieve the video counter person upstairs.

What follows is a dance engaged in many, many times in the course of Louisa's career at the library, a dance always comprised of herself and an unknowing young male partner. As in genuine dancing, there is no real object to its finish. It promises nothing and is twirled through for no sake but its own.

The young man is most likely a student at UT; they usually are, as far as Miss Duffy can ascertain. Students are desirable, though not as laden with erotic taboo as, say, waiters. This particular boy has a scruffy, rather street-like air about him. This is not terribly exciting, but her dance card is, at this hour, empty. Music, Maestro, if you please.

Louisa strides to a neighboring computer; the boy is busily searching on the screen before him. It is doubtful that Miss Duffy will cybernetically locate the item she herself is punching in on the keyboard, as no book on the shelves of Lawson McGhee bears the title, 'I would like to sleep with you'. The content, perhaps, but not the title. Meanwhile the object of her discreetly sideways glancing and the message on her screen seems to have had success in targeting his need. Off to the staircase he goes. Like a supremely confident sprinter, Miss Duffy allows him a ridiculously generous head start. Metaphorically, she is looking at, then lightly blowing upon, her fingernails.

The staircase of the library is spiral, but not free-standing; walls curve to frame it, and these Miss Duffy thinks exceedingly sensual. She likes to run her palms on the walls as she ascends, and never so much as when she knows sensual maleness awaits above.

Emerging onto the second floor, a fast eye and a honed instinct inform her that the boy has in fact turned into the video area. The scene of her fabricated assignment of a few moments earlier; strange, how even small lies are given substance, like mannequins suddenly coming to life.

The rest of the dance is much as the commencement of it. A few steps here by A, a few more angled strategically away taken by B. And the real pleasure for Miss Duffy in this particular ballet lies in the boy's perusing the video shelves. In the purely lusting, yet perversely innocent, dreamscape of Louisa Duffy, the video element is bewitchingly naughty. Lovers watch movies after making love. She rarely extends her reveries beyond the ghostly zipping up of the phantasm's trousers. But, perhaps, another hour would do.

Shortly thereafter the young man rents two tapes, and leaves. Miss Duffy resumes her work as contentedly as she always does. The interrupted song on her lips is once again given whistled form.

No departure can be taken from Louisa Duffy this night, aerially sprite-like or voyeuristically slinking, without an admonition to the watcher of her. Which reads: if there is pity in your breast for her, bestow it elsewhere. If there is a modicum of cruel laughter in the back of your throat, regard the folly of your own existence before you give it voice. For Louisa Duffy does quite all right, thank you. Two of the six thousand idiotic things we humans do pertain strenuously to her, in that we take for granted a wholly illogical and merciful absence of desire in the wretchedly plain, and thereby equip the bad looking with further armor, while happily excising from ourselves the complication of ever looking within to seek what should, as proscribed in the documentation from those few and best of the species, inflame desire to begin with. And the lesser idiot thing of granting epic status to a prolonged state of a very non-epic trait, habit, or inclination. Louisa Duffy, unattractive and old, enjoys the identical, private and never blatantly displayed lust of Louisa Duffy, homely and young. The years have not augmented her desires or the timing of them; nor has the lack of gratification, ever, for them wrought disorders within her brain. They are what they always were, these dreams of sex, and she is what she always was, an occasional dreamer of sex. He who would pity or laugh at this best have inexhaustible fonts of sympathy and gusto to draw upon, if he moves at all in our world.

N I N E

Scenes of Various Domesticities, and a Glimpse of Long Ago

The last day of February. The next day.

If only, John has thought, Knoxville could be walled up in winter. He would be happy. It is then so hauntingly and perfectly *empty*. He thinks this today as he goes, not house-hunting, but house-flirting.

For the horror of the upcoming knee surgery and the tedious repercussions of that morning on Clinch Avenue are about to, if not pay off, pay something. Within the word processors of Gilley, French and Sweet and the insurance agents of Ruth Childress is a figure with a dollar sign before it. Already this sum has been given temporal form, although of an as yet embryonic kind. It will be slapped around a bit by one side, while the other attempts to blow additional girth into it. But these machinations are perfunctory, and all parties concerned either sense or know it. Gossip about a man stopping in the middle of the street, wild talk of something sounding near-suicidal, is not a weapon an insurance agency can wield with any measure of success. Mr. Sweet had in fact thrown upon the table the painful scenario of his client's having been transfixed with fear by the sight of Childress bearing down upon him, and thusly incapable of locomotion.

But this was greeted, not with outrage, but with an irritated sigh. There was no need for it, and the Childress insurance people would have preferred the insult to their intelligence having gone unspoken. Mrs. Childress was a particularly frail variety of senior citizen. There was a stop sign at the corner she was nearing. John Grigio had as pedestrian the right of way. Keep your theatrics, Mr. Sweet, to your Plaza Tower self, thinks the insurance faction. Neither of us needs them.

John is driving this early afternoon. It is not so very bad, driving; he became adroit, and rather quickly, at negotiating both brake and gas pedal with his right foot. His left leg allows itself to be pushed off to the side, like the compliant and less-talented half of a Vaudeville duo. Besides, John drives infrequently: to work, to the Kroger supermarket, on errands. He is a good driver, possibly because he doesn't enjoy it at all. He has observed that the lack of physical consideration so transparent in his fellow creatures when walking upon sidewalks is both masked and exaggerated when they become vehicular. He is not the first to have taken in the contrast. It maddens the average citizen. It is rich fuel to the heart of the misanthrope.

Seamless iron in the Knoxville sky. John drives slowly, slowly; he turns into a certain neighborhood and takes it in as one on foot would, so lazily does he enter it. Fourth and Gill. These are the names at the corner first reached from John's egress off Central Avenue, and he knows of them. Everyone in Knoxville does. They christen not only that corner in the Knoxville mind, but a district, and a district famous for its avenues of what are called Victorian homes. Now, while it is to be safely presumed that, in the eighty-some years to which the lady gave her name, quite a few homes went up in England and in more than one distinctive style, this is America. And in America 'Victorian' translates to fairly large, usually with a porch or veranda, usually in disrepair, and gingerbread. Which translates in any country to something like wooden lace, hideously festooned on eaves.

Here in Knoxville, as in other older neighborhoods in other towns, such homes suffer a fate perverse and ironic; kids, college kids, move into them. These houses often exhibit a rundown aspect, with the concomitant impression of having little left to lose in the way of grandeur vulnerable to careless youth. There are almost always multiple bedrooms and attics, too. If the plumbing isn't ideal and the electrics are antiquated and just safe enough, then the rent is lowered. Which translates to everything in the standard formula for student housing being present.

John peers. He drives at a Childress' pace, and peers. He has never much liked the design of these places. Nor do the imprints of careless youth—a cluster of beer bottles by one curb, skateboards visible behind porch railings as flowerboxes perhaps once were—endear him to this locale. He is not actually *looking* to buy a home, anyway. No check has come his way yet, and the terms of the settlement have not been finalized. And he hadn't much thought of buying a home before the accident. This entire excursion, really, becomes more pointless with his increasing disgust at the robust paraphernalia of the young strewn about these streets.

But every life takes a stroll or a drive three or four times in its duration, only to feel acutely that rising self-annoyance at wasted hours, only to walk or drive to one of the three or four places or people crucial to what it essentially is, or must be. Even cynics, even John. One's whole life is often two streets beyond where the turning off was to be.

He sees the tree first, a beautiful and gnarled old oak. It stands as sentry close to the broken sidewalk, just to the left of the driveway. He thinks, literally, What a great tree. When he inches up a bit more and sees the sign, self-defeatingly obscured behind it. For Sale, Sterling Realty. He carefully pulls in to the narrow drive. As he negotiates this, he has the strongest and most accurate precognition of his life; he will do this same thing many times in the future. He will see the front window from exactly this angle for years. And, at this point, he has not yet actually taken in the house itself.

The yard John carefully steps onto is not unexpectedly overgrown. The entire property, in fact, has a discarded air already by virtue of its placement. On the corner of Gibb and Fifth, there is wonderful distance between it and the neighboring homes: a wide lot occupies a hefty space, room for at least a large house, to its left on Fifth, with a small forest concealing the nearest residence; and Gibb is forlorn, as streets go. The corner itself is an odd juncture born of desperation, a tapering off of habitation. It is a corner people drive to by mistake. It is perfect.

With a silent prayer in his heart John walks to the door, his cane touching broken and ancient flagstone. He looks upward; two stories, quite small. Whatever rooms are within must be modest in dimension, as well. There is a chimney stack to the left. The house is brick. Knowing nothing else, knowing nothing of the state of the facilities inside, whether there is in fact a kitchen which can be saved, whether rodents or termites have staked a claim no deed of ownership can dispel, John knows that this is his house. The moment isn't mystical. But even love isn't mystical.

What it in fact is, what in fact love very often is, is recognition.

*

At six o'clock in the evening of the following day, Alice Ann and Rene are washing their dinner dishes in the kitchen at Pickett Avenue. This is a routine so ritualized to them that juggling with a free hand might be quite naturally looked for from either female.

Alice Ann washes and Rene dries. There is a subtle and potent rationale behind this apportioning of chores, as there is in most kitchens. As Alice Ann perceives herself to be the anchor of the home, she is the one to jump in first, to tackle the wetness and disorder of a task, and to further see these actions as the lion's share of any such household drudgery. Whereas Rene is of the ilk that puts away, tucks in, and straightens. These are not cosmic yins and yangs, but the rhythms are identical, and perhaps as meaningful.

To ensure a semblance of casual interest, Alice Ann has kept her news to herself throughout both the preparing of dinner and the consuming of it. This was not easy, and her eyes had performed a fanatically military examination of every surface in the kitchen as they dined. Now that the final phase of the meal is in full swing, she can proceed. And the props of sponges and plates are good things to have, to enhance the breezy exterior she desires to present to her niece.

"Oh, I almost forgot: has your John mentioned anything lately?"

This is a bit too breezy. Rene wipes water from a glass and says, "Mentioned anything?"

"I just thought he might've told you his big news." Quite unintentionally, Alice Ann has made the leap from insouciant to catty, in the space of a few scant seconds.

Rene is not spiteful, but she does have a sense of fun. "You know, I think we should go back to Dove. The suds are better, too." The understood attribute of the soap resides in its legendary softness, to both women and to all of America.

"Rene. Do you know what I'm talking about, or don't you."

"No, Alice Ann. I don't."

"All *right*, then." Alice Ann's hands repeatedly and briskly extend their fingers, to eject excess dishwater. She looks like a magician trying frantically to conjure a rabbit out of the sink. "Well. It seems Carolyn got a call today to show a house. To a Mr. *Grigio*."

Rene does not attempt to feign disinterest. Her aunt for various reasons invokes John in their home for various purposes, and she knows that. But, as this is inscrutable conduct to Rene, there is little to be gained by trying to fathom what is underneath each instance and then respond accordingly. So she reacts as she normally would.

"Really? Wow."

"Wow?"

"That's great. Is it a nice house?"

Now, Alice Ann, even in her most subconsciously Machiavellian ideas about John and what may be his intentions regarding her niece, has thus far never actually entertained the prospect of a real union between them. Nonetheless. Perhaps it is time she does. For this question from Rene, so innocent, hits her like a thunderbolt. Somewhere in Alice Ann a voice is crying out: nice? How can you not be mortified that he'd buy a house without consulting you?

"I don't know that I'd call it *nice*."

Rene is puzzled. "Well, it can't be too awful. John's pretty smart, and he's got great taste."

Alice Ann then mentally connects homosexuality and a discerning eye, adding a square to the quilt of John's gross unsuitability she knits in her spare time. "Well, Carolyn–she's handling the property–isn't very impressed. It's kind of a white elephant, on the books for years. Small, run-down, in the middle of nowhere."

"Nowhere? It's in Knoxville, isn't it?"

"Too small for a real *family*."

"Is it in Knoxville, Alice Ann?"

"Oh, of course. Honey, Sterling's handling it, after all. But it's on some awful little corner in the Fourth and Gill area."

Rene almost laughs. The sound she in fact makes is the common one of a single expulsion of breath, to suggest disbelief at a recently expressed and ridiculous exaggeration of the facts. "Oh, Alice Ann. 'Nowhere'."

"You know what I mean, dear. Nowhere *nice*."

"There are nice homes in that neighborhood. I've seen them."

"Yes, but Carolyn…well, she knows what she's talking about. And she doesn't seem to think anyone in their right mind would want the place."

Alice Ann's usage of Carolyn's name in their dialogue is nearly litigiously wrong. She is employing it to emphasize that sisterly bond the two women at Sterling Realty most emphatically do not share. For this is what had occurred in the office:

Alice Ann had been at her desk, in the process of transferring a caller to the voice mail of an absent salesperson. With one ear she had been listening, albeit distractedly, to Carolyn's call at her own desk. Alice Ann's attention had been gripped, suddenly, by hearing her unattainable colleague say, "I'll see you then, Mr. Grigio."

At which point Alice Ann made no pretense of idle curiosity. What she did was worse. She flew to Carolyn's desk unthinkingly confident in the power of the association just then established between them. She, Alice Ann, had an interest in John Grigio; her niece worked for him and was perhaps in love with him. Now this very man was engaged in purchasing a home through her own agency. That Carolyn and she would be made as one by this was an irrefutable side benefit to whatever transaction Mr. Grigio was contemplating, and a foregone conclusion to boot. So she flew to Carolyn's desk with a Grigio dossier, to barter for the facts of this Grigio deal.

Carolyn's eyes had expanded to meet Alice Ann's in a reflex of realtor greeting. "Yes, Alice Ann?" Who placed her hands on her hips, adopting the one feminine pose possessed of every possible meaning.

"I couldn't help but hear, Carolyn. Did you say, 'Mr. Grigio'?"

"Why, yes, I did. A new client, dear."

At this alone, Alice Ann seethes within her voluptuous frame. New client. No kidding, she thought. Good Lord, I practically *run* this office.

"Well, it's just so *funny*, Carolyn. He's the man…my Rene works with him."

"Does she, now?"

You are a bitch, a miserable bitch, thought Alice Ann. She did not, strangely, pause to wonder why she continually sought the woman's favor and friendship.

"Oh, yes. He's the boy who got badly hurt in that accident last fall." Carolyn offered nothing, not a crumb, in response. "My Rene's been I suppose his best friend since."

Below Carolyn's brunette coif: Well, aren't you the Goddamn Queen of Knoxville. What she said was, "I see. Rene is such a doll."

Oh!, exploded in Alice Ann's brain. Oh, bee-itch!

"So, when I heard you say his name, naturally I wondered."

At this point Carolyn relented. She never despised Alice Ann, never thought ill of her, except when Alice Ann cozied up to her. As Alice Ann actually admired Carolyn, until Carolyn's haughtiness went up like a flag.

The women would be the greatest of friends, if only they could refrain from contact. However, then, Carolyn foresaw that denying Alice Ann the basic information she so badly craved would serve only to keep her, simpering, nearby.

"Well. John Grigio is very interested in Lot 202. The Gibb and Fifth house."

"*That* place? Lord, we've had that on the books for years."

"Well. He seems taken with it, from what I could tell."

At this Alice Ann froze, thwarted in what should have been a natural progress. There was so much she could confidentially impart, impressions of John and her own worries over her niece's fondness for him, to a friend. And there were people within the walls of Sterling to whom she could comfortably convey these anxieties. But she wanted Carolyn, as the unnoticed suitor lets go to waste his love, saving it for the one who wants no part of it.

But Carolyn had frozen too, and in a less complicated way. She might not have slapped away an outstretched hand, but she would not have clasped it. And that would be far worse.

"Well, then. I'll have to talk to Rene. Interesting, don't you think?"

Carolyn thought it possibly the least interesting item in a dull day, and said, "Oh, yes." Alice Ann smiled painfully and retreated to her own desk, prompted by an outrageously supercilious nod from Carolyn. Who was thinking, God help that poor niece.

Thusly had Alice Ann obtained her facts.

Back in the kitchen on Pickett, the dishes are done. Rene is preparing the coffee maker, a kiddie version of her daily brewing downtown. Alice Ann is wiping the counter, the sink, the faucet, everything.

"Whatever your friend says, I know John. If he's really going to buy a house, I'm sure it's a nice house. Or will be."

Alice Ann wrings the water from her dish towel with both hands. She has an impulse to slip her hands into her hair, grab hold of it, and pull. But she does not do this.

*

When John was a boy…No.

When John Grigio was very young, he was precocious. Certain children have been of course labeled as such since the first youngster declined the invitation to join the elders in pursuit of dinner, currently tusked and mobile in the surrounding wood, in favor of the solitude of the cave and the gratification of the stone tablet and flint marker. That has never helped. Eon may straddle eon of such mysterious and unsettling refusals, and no wisdom has generationally been imbedded in the DNA of the species which makes the affair more explicable and less shameful to the parents, be they atavistic or thoroughly modern. The parents take comfort in the probability that the child will eventually wield the sort of influence that renders football a matter of buying and selling men. But that is still comfort, and comfort is taken because something is not right.

So John was not exactly a boy, and he displayed egghead tendencies, and Mr. and Mrs. Grigio found solace in the aforementioned hope of the future killings made by little eggheads, and in whiskey.

The family lived in a rather nice neighborhood in the middle of the vast reaches of New York State. And there is small need to deeply examine their house or its inhabitants. John was cared for, but not excessively so, as his early maturity coincided agreeably with his parents' increasing inability to tend anything at all. They were not violent or disruptive drinkers, the Grigios. If they never exhibited a great deal in the way of interest in their son, they did not abuse him, nor was he neglected in the basic necessities. In point of fact the distilled cloud in which they passed their own lives worked, in some fashion, to John's advantage. For requests by him for articles not ordinarily asked for by young boys–such as books–failed to trigger in them a determination to alter the course of interest displayed many another parent would seize upon as a parental duty. As whiskey let the elder Grigios go their own way, it allowed their issue to march to whichever drummer he heard.

John's mother and father still live, still consume fiendishly, and still occupy the house in New York. John telephones them every two weeks.

He sometimes travels for badly-cooked holiday meals. It is on these occasions and on these occasions alone that John will assert his claim to a Grigio throne, and drink an awful lot. In his defense, the Grigio refrigerator boasts no liquids not of the mixing variety. And his parents don't care for juice concoctions.

That was, and is, Grigio House. Modest, comfortable, sloppily sentimental or not speaking to itself. It was the house in which John sat cross-legged on the floor before the RCA console model and watched the world Hollywood beat into shape in the 1930's and 1940's. It was where his room was, and where he studied. It was where he first thought of rescue, but only by his own hands. Even then, he had no illusions that other houses were better. Even then, he observed that real people were not quite behaving themselves as they ought to. When John dreamt of rescue, he dreamt of dreamy solitude.

Two things beyond this call for notice:

John's psyche, within youngster and man, was and is imperious. But few psyches reign absolutely over all territories, and lust is a notoriously tough outpost. Lust usually conquers all temporarily, its nobler cousin of love laying claim to more permanent residency. Call the fantasies of young men romance, or employ seasonal metaphor to pretty up the glandular explosions; howsoever named, they are preeminent in youth. Even for the egghead. Yet the outcome of the battle within young John could well be anybody's guess. John's nascent cynicism in adolescence was already, like a potent weed, choking more conventional desires. His budding jaundiced vision was unwilling to step back, to make room for primal urges. John, even young John, didn't trust people. Thus lust was an annoyance to be dealt with only when unavoidably required. And love, which encompasses to a certain degree involvement with another…No. Love was not a thing to harbor. The other aspect of John calling for attention is remarkable. It will be evident later in his life, in his story.

*

As technicians skilled in detecting signs of life in frozen or inert matter hear what the lay ear may not, we see stirrings in the paralyzed landscape of February. They are moreover localized; in the deceptively icy stillness of the entire Fourth and Gill neighborhood, there are rustlings to be noted in more than one house.

Kimberly Stritch rents a Victorian house on Fourth itself. The rent is not high by the standards of the working class, but it is rather steep in the residually allowanced minds of college students. So Kim needed a roommate, Kim posted the need on various boards around the University of Tennessee campus, and Kim got, as an ordinary person walking down an ordinary street makes one bad step and plunges into a manhole, Andrea. It is a thing to be grateful for, that most of us will never take so subterranean and dark a journey. Kim's major at UT is economics, with a minor in social sciences. Courtesy of Andrea, the field of study with which she is most immersed is that of aberrant, or deviant, psychology.

On this February afternoon Kim is in her bedroom. It is very like Kim itself, in that it echoes a decade long past. The ponytail of its mistress' hair, the slacks and little flat slippers she often wears, even the twinkle in her eye suggesting mischief below an Eisenhower exterior, are redolent of the 1950's. As the room itself bespeaks a modestly contained aspect of girlish vivacity, by means of a few posters of a few of the more non-militant musical bands of the current year, and the even more ingenuous touches of a hill of hair clips on a dressing table and a troop of satin-padded hangers in her closet. If the musical suggestion to twist again is not heard in this room, it ought to be.

But today, this hour, is not one for giddy gyrating. Kim has on her pink bedspread a collection of bills strewn before her, and in her hand is the carefully arrived upon summation of all that black and white. It substantiates what she has known for five of the six months Andrea has shared the house. Namely, that Andrea is annoyingly guilty of paying less than her half of the utilities, and far less than the long distance phone calls she has contributed to that particularly outrageous bill.

How has this gone on so long? The answer is now fully clear to Kim, and points to something worse than a deadbeat. She clearly comprehends at last, now, the corkscrew machinations of Andrea: how she will commendably hand Kim a short stack of notes ahead of time for an amount of oil not yet calculated by its supplier; how she similarly and deficiently pays in advance for electricity days before its assessment; and how stunned, blatantly stunned, is her reaction to the fingernail of Kim just below a twenty dollar phone call to Florida. So profound is the manifestation of Andrea's disbelief at such figures, in fact, that Kim has paused in her own sanity and considered the possibility of an unseen and highly communicative squatter on the premises.

But, no more. Confrontation is distasteful to Kim—a sensibility Andreae can sniff out as hummingbirds do nectar—but this will be resolved. She hears the front door and, armed with facts and paper, steps out to meet her duplicitous roommate. Had Kim taken a history major, she might have been better prepared to face the bitter and historically cascaded truth of the too frequent impotence of right.

Andrea is breathlessly pleased. She darts to the kitchen, darts to the refrigerator. Kim enters the room to see her gulping down juice from the carton.

"Hi. God, my job sucks. You know they won't let me drink *juice* there?" This is untrue. Andrea had once been gently scolded by Rene for chugging a glass in front of a customer. In the mind of an Andrea, facts are beautifully elastic.

"Really."

"Yep." Andrea wipes her mouth with her hand. Then the sickly green glow of her essence flares; there is danger here. This she knows, without even noticing the papers in Kim's hand.

"Andrea, I need to talk to you about the bills."

It is a shame that thousands pay large amounts for theater tickets to see what is pedestrian fare, when the sort of real artistry about to shine in that kitchen goes unviewed. Andrea is good. She is so good that, rather than adopt the pretense of having no time to discuss the matter–despite a strong desire to do so–she takes the entire scene into her powerful little hands and turns it upside down.

"OK. Absolutely. Let's sit down."

Kim complies, uneasily drawing out a chair for herself.

"All right. I hate to bring it up, but this thing of you giving me money before the bills come just isn't working."

"No?" Andrea's eyes are pools of distress.

"No. I mean, I appreciate it, but the bills are always more and I make up the difference."

"God, I'm sorry. I was trying to make it easier for you."

"Right. But–well, look at this." She places before Andrea's rapt eyes the last fuel bill. "See? Seventy-nine. A week before it came, you gave me twenty-five."

Andrea looks long and hard at the document. She is of course not seeing it. There are at the moment several avenues open to her. These, she sees. On the very deepest plane of what she is, this experience is being registered by her as further training.

"I see it. I'll get it to you; Friday's tips are the best." Then, before Kim has a chance to confirm or reject this sketchy offer, *voila*. Andrea turns to the fabrication she had planned to unveil later, slaps a great deal of plaster on it and, with a flourish and a swirl of opera cloak, swipes away the canvas cover. "But, you know what?"

Kim is somewhat numbed already. She is mortified at having thought that an unpleasant clash would occur and be seen through by her. She is ashamed of having left her bedroom and not having foreseen acquiescence in the shape of more lies. "What?"

Andrea shows many small, white teeth. "I may be moving out soon."

Up, up, goes Kim. Andrea is a giantess, tossing Kim into the air like a ball. "Really?"

"Uh-huh." The game hers, Andrea returns to the refrigerator to drink more juice in easy and not at all premature triumph. "I met a *guy*."

The ascent of Kim is halted. She is stuck airborne, like a cartoon of herself. "I didn't want to tell you before we settled it yet. But he's so cool."

Cartoon Kim's eyes look down to see the caricature of spikes below.

"His name's *Rodney*. He's so sweet." This will live on as one of six absolutely true remarks made by Andrea in the entire course of her peripatetic and false life. "He came to the restaurant last month and asked me out. It's moving pretty fast, but it's great."

Kim's arms flail at the air, and her legs pedal furiously.

"That's great, really. So...you're moving in with him?"

"Well, he asked me, the last time I saw him. I said I'd think about it."

Kim, falling.

Then Andrea delivers the masterstroke, in referring to the topic she so deftly sidled around. "But, don't worry. I'll give you plenty of notice. And I'll get that money to you next week." The door on the Maytag slams, more teeth are flashed, and Andrea is gone. Leaving Kim bruised by an assortment of hits to her esteem in her own intelligence; with further bills not even gone into; and with the sadness of this last, fresh lie, that of Andrea's potential vacating. For Kim has not yet met Rodney, but she knows. She knows that no offer was made. She knows that she may as well have the locks changed while the girl is at work than mention again this fantasy, so cataclysmic would be the result of the truth being spoken and Andrea's denial of it. And she doesn't know but can guess that, if this Rodney is indeed pondering a move after dating Andrea, it is likely one to a foreign shore, and unaccompanied.

Ten

A Retrospective Travelogue, in Which Spite Temporarily Dozes

John walked into Garamond's for the first time in April of 1992. This, four days after his arrival in town.

He had not so much decided to settle in Knoxville, Tennessee, as he had run out of gas. This being John, there was more than a modicum of premeditation to this recklessness. That is, he had not so much run out of gas as he had foreseen where an empty tank would leave him. Having no specific destination in mind, he thought a dual strategy his best bet. He would scout for a suitable town with an urgency in proportion to his dwindling gas supply. The lower the tank, the more intent would be his scanning. As a last resort, he would compromise and retrace his vehicular steps, if what appeared to be his final destination also appeared to be a frightening one.

Why south? Why did he not elect to pursue a western, or even more eastern, course?

Hard to say, really. It may be that his hometown of Newkirk was so far north and so far east as to make further exploration in those directions less than enticing. It can be averred with certainty that the West, near or

Californian, held not one iota of fascination for him. And, as the real object was to settle somewhere a respectable distance *away*, that left only one avenue open.

So he drove for two days. He saw the signs proclaiming the lessening distance to Knoxville as soon as he crossed the Tennessee state line, from West Virginia. All of West Virginia had been quite out of the question. It wasn't that John shared in the derision enjoyed by the rest of the union for that particularly lambasted state; on the contrary, such underdog status enhanced most anything in his mind. If most of humanity mocks it, it can't be so bad. However. There were the crosses. At intervals on I-81 were cryptic and disturbing trios of large crosses, all the way through West Virginia. They may have denoted the predominant religious persuasion of the counties so staked, or they may have carried a helpful message of some kind to the iconically well-informed. But to John they suggested something ritualistic, something painful undergone for the sake of a greater good, and something not at all inviting. So, to Tennessee.

Like most cities accessible by highway, Knoxville broadcasts its nearness by means of an exponentially multiplying number of motels. So many Days Inns and Holiday Inns and Red Roof Inns; clearly, the world frequently unpacks here for a night or two. These augurs of intense life did not discourage John. He was unimpressed by size and urban trumpeting, and took it in automotive stride. Nor did the billboards proclaiming the sheer rightness of the town so soon to unfold before him pique much in the way of his interest. Advertising, he knew, for a city or for soup, was advertising, and nothing more.

But, as every mile on I-40 took him closer to the heart of the city, an odd thing happened: he believed it all, while disbelieving all its shabby promotion. It seemed as though Knoxville was exactly the right place–he had not even entered it yet–not because of the hoopla, but in spite of it. As a lie will reveal a truth. In spite of itself.

So into Knoxville he rolled, knowing he would stay as he made his first foray into the city proper. Rather than pull into the Radisson hotel so convenient and so lordly on Summit Hill Avenue, he relaxed and breathed in the full luxury of a burden discharged. This would be his home; the search was done. A little scouting, then, a little driving in circles, might break the ice of foreign territory. It took no great logistical reckoning to determine that the center of the city lay to the south of where he was, so John swung a lazy right onto Gay Street. Nothing he saw was in any way compelling, or even worthy of a second glance. There were glazed and lifeless store fronts, a fast food outlet, a bank, an old theatre. Nothing. A somewhat jazzy optometrist's suite, parking lots, and a stencil on a window proclaiming the site of Slomski's Tailors, the dusty and chipped lettering of it proclaiming more vehemently the lack behind them of any activity at all for perhaps decades. Nothing, and less than nothing of Slomski.

John turned onto Cumberland, establishing it as pretty much the southern barrier to the downtown, and was not disappointed in what he saw as he was in no way impressed by the same. Not even by that which so cries out to be taken in, the Whittle building, two blocks of prim Georgian façade housing, just then, the excitement of an empire on the rise and not the panic of its soon to be exiled founders a few years hence. It was handsome, as sprawling buildings go; but gave off too strongly a sensibility of itself as nice looking, as nice looking people may do. He skirted the side of the library on Walnut Street and an odd little lawyer's townhouse opposite to it, and decided then to immerse himself further into these untried waters. Before even settling upon a hotel. He decided to take a space in the lot before him, buy a local newspaper and, with every step amiably but firmly declaring his advent to Knoxville, stroll.

So did John Grigio stroll, in the late afternoon of an overcast day in late April of 1992. His soul was open, as receptive as it knew how to be. This was a city, people were involved, and thusly no real good could be reasonably presumed to be on its streets. But he had never been in the South before. Everyone insisted that Southerners were different, and maybe the difference was in their being less like what people were elsewhere. This was John's hope.

It was confirmed by his taking his newspaper and a container of coffee into Krutch Park, which revealed itself to him as the most suitable place in which to take in the town for a few minutes, before his senses would overflow with the newness of it all and the safety of a hotel room would be essential. The confirmation was exposed to him aurally, by means of the following words passed between an old man and a not so elderly woman:

"She don't care." This, from the woman.

"You don't know that, mother."

"Don't I, though?"

"She likes you well enough."

"Not as I see it."

"You are far too critical of spirit, mother."

That was all John heard, and his heart sang at it. The exchange came to his ears as poetry, filled with idiomatic terseness and grace. He did not hear it as a bad-tempered woman's commonplace obstinacy, received by a passive partner. John wields perception of a very high order, as has been noted. But he was walking on ground virgin to him, ground he wanted to make a home, and his stopping in the park launched his soul's mechanisms of a distinctly selective receptivity. It is not unreasonable to suppose that his discerning eye sought under the circumstances more pleasing shapes, and that his ears listened only for harmonies. So does a man inclined for an evening's company overlook the transparency of the wig on the woman at the adjacent bar stool.

With the happy omen of the fragment of overheard and gorgeously Southern conversation behind him, John was emboldened. Gray days were lucky for him, anyway, another augur. He walked on surer legs back to Gay; at Summit Hill, he dimly noticed the interesting halo of the Old City neighborhood at its base, and continued thusly. The town was endearing itself to him further with each new step, by its delightful accessibility for the walker. He wanted to buy the city a drink.

He made his way on Central, through the heart of the Old City, if so marginal an area may be said to require so muscular an organ. He looked into shop windows and was pleased to see a vast amount of what had to be Southern debris. He did not take in that the milk glass lamps were of a manufacture seen throughout the nation; they were there, and bore for John the imprint of Confederate tradition. He quite looked forward to learning about his new home. He would never be a Southerner, but it was agreeable to think that he might, in time, be a respected Yankee.

Too bad, that we rarely gather up our fool's gold and go home with it. Too bad, that the desirous man in the bar will forget himself and attempt to pass his hand through waves of his new companion's false hair.

John swung open a somewhat tarnished brass door and entered a sort of café on Jackson. The place was clean, smartly done up in an Art Deco style, and absolutely huge. One other customer sat within, nursing something from a coffee cup the size of a fruit bowl. John took a discreet little table tucked by a wall, and waited. A young woman in an apron saw him from behind the pastry case she was tending. John saw her see him, and presented to her his best, subtle and friendly, nod.

The girl returned this silent greeting by furrowing her brow in mild surprise mixed with a dash of annoyance. And she made no hasty move to accommodate the new guest. She made in fact no move at all save the continued wiping with one hand of a whisk held in the other. In the stillness of the café, John's generous outlook of the hour past began to button its coat and put on its hat, as it were.

Yet there was nothing to do but sit, and wait a bit more. Perhaps, he reasoned, the girl needed time to fully take in the reality of his presence. Perhaps, he more sarcastically wondered, she had wasted too many trips from the counter on customer mirages. So he made his innocent stand by sitting, and perused on a menu card all the items he was apparently not worthy to receive.

"We're not really open." This from the girl, who had finally chosen the compromise of leaving her former position but not quite coming all the way up to John's table.

"Oh," said John, and he cannot be blamed for it. There was quite literally nothing else to say, and surely more by way of explanation would follow from his hostess.

"No." That was it. It was not, in the girl's defense, spoken harshly. But there was a sense that he was taking valuable time and attention away from the whisk she still polished.

Still wanting to be receptive, still wanting things to be nice, John smiled affably. "I didn't know. Your door *is* open…" He said this to give as much as he could. Maybe his entry had been unobserved by this girl; maybe she hadn't yet drawn a line connecting his unwelcome physicality with a mistakenly unlocked door.

Then the last vestiges of a salvageable niceness dissolved into, not air, but the acid of what had been too much of John's experience of life. Because the girl raised her eyes in clear dismissal of his observation as completely pointless. As though open doors to businesses invariably implied invitation. Really, now. The girl shook her head in exasperation at his naivete, and the whisk shone like a crude weapon in the hands of a meticulously clean cave housewife.

"Yeah. Fine." He rose and said upon leaving, "You might want to think about locking the door. Or turning off the lights, or something." He did not present this instruction rudely, but there was no escaping a patronizing tone. But delivery was irrelevant, as was message. The whisk, John saw, was everything.

So it was that within two hours of first arriving in Knoxville, John Grigio had taken it to his heart, been a little moved by its persona, and reviled it as yet another outpost of blatant incivility and staggering idiocy. His new home. He checked into the Hilton.

Eleven

A Pause for Subterfuge

A picturesque scene of Mrs. Childress baking and Mrs. Ansley talking.

It is early March of 1997, and early in the day. Ellen Ansley has stopped by uninvited for coffee with her friend. The incident is not without precedent. But it catches Ruth Childress blushingly unawares. The pie just placed in her oven is to be another gift of home manufacture to John Grigio, the sixth in a sequence of something she keeps needing to do. The others were all rolled, fluted, pricked with a fork like an old woman's charade of a stabbing murder, and sent off on the momentum of each previous offering. But this one is now as weighty and potentially pivotal as the first, as imbued with almost as much complicated meaning as its rhubarb predecessor had been, on the counter of Garamond's. The surprise presence of her friend changes things. The women could talk over coffee and sweet biscuits, but the unfinished pie and its destination must be withheld from Mrs. Ansley. Therefore the pie is treacherous, an open diary. If Mrs. Ansley learns of the pie, Ruth fears she will be unable to conceal the whole truth of it from her. Ruth must exercise great care, lest her natural honesty reveal too much and draw her friend's inevitable disapproval. From the very beginning of this business with John Grigio, Ellen Ansley had viewed it as an audacious young man's rolling of a helpless widow. Well, the widow was not helpless. The widow had Mrs. Ansley in her corner.

A pie doesn't belong to the melodrama of the meek being taken by the wily. Pies belong to burlesque. Ruth must hide the fact of the pie, to better protect its purpose.

So they chat like two elderly women, one of whom knows there is a body behind the sofa and one of whom would swear she spies a heel protruding from that region.

Mrs. Ansley picks up Ruth's copy of the newspaper on the table. She knows already its contents. "Did you see that ass' latest brilliance?" The ass in question is a city councilman not respected by Mrs. Ansley.

"Did I?" Ruth is slightly flustered. She brushes telltale bits of dough from the counter with a dish cloth. "I'm sure I did. Fitz-something, isn't it?"

Ellen Ansley emits a modest raspberry in derision. "Fitzwilliam, Ruth. Oh, that jackass." She is not hard of feature, Mrs. Ansley. She is in fact a softer version of the softly pretty girl she was, with additional and not unflattering folds here and there on her face, like well-placed draperies. It is only in her expression, in her eyes, that the hardness resides. That is what people who know her for any length of time see. It is said that intelligence destroys the beauty of a face; force of character simply plows through it.

"He *said*, Ruth, that 'Tennessee seniors need special care'." She pauses, to allow this outrage to penetrate fully into her friend's consciousness. "Special care. That patronizing, impudent *jack*ass."

Ruth stands with her back to the oven, her little doll arms folded over her chest, in a posture of studied nonchalance. "Ellen. I'm sure he meant well."

"Oh, like hell." The pleasant half-circles of Mrs. Ansley's nostrils twitch. "Ruth, what do I smell?"

The more truthful the soul, the more laughable its tries at deceit. Ruth feigns surprise at this very badly indeed, which means she registers something like shock. "Smell, dear?"

"Yes, Ruth. Smell. Are you baking?"

"No."

Astonishingly, this is accepted by Mrs. Ansley. Well, why not? Ruth Childress does not lie. Mrs. Ansley peers at the newsprint once again, determined to isolate for her friend further phrases damning the ass Fitzwilliam. "Let me see…Oh. Here. Listen to this. 'After all, they are our parents. We can't just hope they'll go away.' Go away. Ass."

Inspiration strikes Mrs. Childress. She reaches into the cabinet below her sink for an air freshener she had purchased and does not care for. The hiss of the aerosol can, however, hinders the greater design. For it draws the attention of Mrs. Ansley away from the newspaper. Who is now staring at her little friend, who is using both her little hands to wield a spray can for no earthly reason.

Mrs. Childress is aware of being scrutinized. So she cunningly decides to volunteer a false explanation, believing the initiative will further its credibility. She says too loudly, "I burned tarts this morning. Couldn't you smell it, Ellen?"

Mrs. Ansley is slow to respond. She is hypnotized by the pendulum swing of the can in Ruth's hands, back, forth, back, forth. "No. I couldn't." Her gaze remains level. "Did you say 'tarts', Ruth?"

"Yes." The hissing ceases. The kitchen is perfumed with something like the scent of many gardenias soaking in molten steel. "Tarts. *Lemon* tarts."

Mrs. Ansley's eyes water. She says, passing the newspaper before her face like a fan, "Well, no one would know it, now. Lord, Ruth." Yet the ridiculous subterfuge works because, as before, it is more reasonable to suppose that Mrs. Childress burned tarts, drastically overreacted and attacked the field of her disgrace with synthetic scent, than to think she would lie. However. There is an element of suspicion in Mrs. Ansley's eyes. Ruth Childress sees it, but does not know that it is born from her old friend's growing concern that the car accident of last year did something to her own psyche. Ruth is horrified to think that somehow, despite no trace of crust left on the counter and through a blistering fog of metallic gardenia, Mrs. Ansley senses a lemon meringue pie in the oven.

"The thing I find most objectionable," begins Mrs. Ansley, and Ruth thinks, What? The lemon, the egg whites, what?, "is the ass referring to us as though we're a guilty ...burden. To dis*charge*." This is well said, and Mrs. Ansley is pleased with herself. She will remember her phrasing and employ it again at a town meeting. Where she is largely respected, not as a senior citizen, not as a combatively intelligent senior citizen, but because she has money.

Ruth breathes in deeply with relief and chokes a bit on the sickly fragrance.

"Are you all right, dear?"

"Yes. Fine, really." A thin coating of My Garden household room freshener remains on the roof of her mouth. "What were you saying?"

This visit is peculiar, thinks Mrs. Ansley, and best ended. She rises from the table, and Ruth Childress deploys her little body once more as a shield to the oven door furiously warming her lower half. A last stand.

"Call me later, won't you?" Ruth throws this out as a sop. Then Mrs. Ansley moves toward her. She eyes Mrs. Childress indulgently and skeptically, and suddenly puts her arms around her. "You take care of yourself now, will you? I'll call later."

The embrace is released and Mrs. Ansley goes to the door. Safety is a scant few seconds away. Then she turns, sniffs again, and says, "Hm. I *do* smell lemon." Then she leaves.

Ruth Childress waits to hear the door close before she removes her posterior from the now dangerously heated position it has occupied. And she is crimson in the face from, not the oven, but shame.

Twelve

Miss Marchbanks, Money, and Refreshments

Miss Marchbanks is by no means the dragon of Gilley, Sweet and French. Nor does the title 'receptionist' do her justice. To be painfully honest, she is the aging and silly *premiere vendeuse* of the legal firm.

How very absurd must have been the ingenue Miss Marchbanks, years past, when first she presided over the telephones and appointment books of her employers. Her speech was naïve and countrified then, as it is now, and the friendly vacancy in her large green eyes was empty of the patina of authority age gives to even the most vacant expressions. As it is today. Age has failed to work its authoritative spell, and the absurdity of the young Miss Marchbanks has merely evolved into the greater improbability of the elder Miss Marchbanks. She had ribbons in her hair when she began her career, and newer ribbons adorn it still, tied into bows around gray pigtails. In her early days with the firm she must have looked like a schoolgirl come to visit an uncle, who then stepped around the desk to answer a telephone no one else was hearing. In a sense, that is how she began her job. Thirty years later the telephone still rings and she still speaks into it with the teen contralto and rural vernacular still in her possession.

Times, of course, change, even around that which only ages and does not otherwise alter. Grainger Gilley, he who had founded the firm and hired Miss Marchbanks–that is, seen her behind the front desk one day and began giving her paychecks a week later— is dead. Associates have come and gone; a few have tried to replace Miss Marchbanks with someone more appropriate to the dignity of the legal profession she represents. Which is in essence the dignity of wood paneling, and fear. Ah, but Miss Marchbanks goes nowhere. Like Cosimo de Medici, she has seen fall those who would bring her down. She is as immovable as the massive portrait of Gilley looking approvingly, if watchfully, down upon her. There has been speculation that her unaccountable longevity with the office is in fact linked preternaturally to the picture.

Times change. A computer was built into the reception desk of Gilley, French and Sweet several years earlier. Those who think Miss Marchbanks a fool might revise their opinion, if they knew that she has yet to master one single function of the modern marvel at her disposal. And no one, not even those who would depose her, know this. Below the computer is a thin shelf, and on it is Miss Marchbanks' book. And in this book she jots down the cybernetic needs of the associates actually willing to entrust her with them, and at the end of each day she brings the book to Sir Speedy, on the plaza level of the building, and has the arcane work done for her. In a roundabout variation on computer dating, she has begun stepping out with the middle-aged and equally rustic manager of Sir Speedy. Who is savvy with computers and yet susceptible to the charms of those who are not.

Carry on, Miss Marchbanks. You do nothing much, but you do no real harm.

On the fifth of April, John presses his stick deep into the carpet of the 20th floor to better anchor himself as he swings open the thick oak door of Gilley, French and Sweet. Today is the day. Today, all renumerations arising from the unfortunate accident are to be settled. Three weeks before, March 20th was the day as well, as John had undergone then the knee surgery so vaguely prognosticated, then more pragmatically performed, by Dr. Perkey. Tucked between John's ribcage and right arm is a thin leather sheaf, and in it are papers which blandly divine a lifelong handicap.

The left hand of Miss Marchbanks shoots up in warning as he approaches; she is on the telephone and seemingly fears that he cannot see this, and will speak. In fairness to Miss Marchbanks, that has actually, if infrequently, occurred with other visitors, and she has been unable then to take in either telephonic or organic request.

"Gilley, French and Sweet?", John hears her say. He has himself been the object of this announcement by her over the phone, and notes once more the woman's extraordinary syllabic emphasis: as uttered by Miss Marchbanks, the second two names become randy adjectives of the first, promising a sexy and Gallic Gilley.

John waits politely, resting on his stick. He does not eavesdrop, but the fragments of conversation he can't avoid hearing indicate that, somewhere in Knoxville, someone is holding his phone receiver away from his face and staring at it in open-mouthed wonder. Miss Marchbanks hangs up the phone and then asks John, whom she has spoken with seven times through that very implement and once in person, who he is and whom he wishes to see. It should be noted that she performs this exercise and reveals the sweeping vista of her incapacity in a chipper and friendly way.

"Right..." The mouth of Miss Marchbanks extends this word mercilessly; stretches it on the rack, as it were, and screws its single vowel into an 'a'. She turns a leaf in her appointment book, expresses shock, then turns it back and forth once again. From this John deduces that Miss Marchbanks was on the wrong day, and that this may have been responsible for the telephonic confusion of a minute earlier. Giddy with merriment at her own folly, she cries, "I'll *be*!" Although this hits the air as 'I'll *bay*', John understands. And thinks, Yes, you'll be. You'll always be, won't you, you imbecile?

Minutes pass. John occupies them in speculating upon who could so desperately require representation as to leap this bumpkin hurdle each time. Then he realizes: as he himself is doing. Oh, whale.

Fifteen minutes later John is seated at a surprisingly small and dainty table in the firm's conference room. He has not seen this room before; it is amazing. It is so un-lawyerish as to make an occupant second guess his elevator button choice. The walls aren't paneled but papered, and papered in pastel bluebells. There are shelves, but they are barren of legal texts and instead support porcelain shepherdesses. There is furniture, but it is upholstered in florals. And the pictures on the bluebelled walls are not likenesses of attorneys past, but birds. Without even an owl, to lend legal nuance.

Whence such defiantly unlawful décor? Whence else, but from the spacious realm between the ribbons above Miss Marchbanks' ears. The room had at one time been the sort of room one would anticipate, with wood and leather as its landscape. Miss Marchbanks is no sorceress; the changes brought about in consonance to her own taste did not occur overnight. However: twelve years before, when the paneling needed replacing, the breach into the camp of severity was made, and Marchbanks marched. As the bluebells went up, the leather wrinkled, recoiling in fear, and the worn and deep green carpet knew its monotonous tenure could not long survive. The Chesterfield sofa stared long and hard at the stately conference table, as the man with one foot on the scaffold steps looks to the fellow nearer to the rope. The table did indeed buckle and fall. And the sofa, assaulted by the bluebells on every side, found that the addition of Delphiniums on the new carpet below its claws made extinction a welcome prospect. During these painful transmutations, there were those employed at Gilley, French and Sweet who coughed a lot when each fresh batch of flowers went up and went down. The coughing even became a pronounced hacking when the birds took their cue to alight. But the portrait of Grainger Gilley in the foyer never doesn't not look down upon Miss Marchbanks, or her seat. The protection of the woman by the portrait is of course theoretical, at best. It gains its power only through the supposition that it just may have it. In human affairs, forever, that has always been enough.

John looks about him and correctly thinks, Miss Marchbanks. Yet a strange benefit to the firm is had by this very slap to its dignity. Its

outrageousness serves to combat unease, and that is no small thing in a
lawyers' suite.

As John enters he immediately sees Mrs. Childress, brilliantly old lady-
like in an overstuffed chair, her little legs crossed at her littler ankles, her
sparkling hands folded in her lap. It takes minimal sensitivity on John's
part to know how she has been looking at the door prior to his advent,
awaiting it. He goes to a loveseat—yes, a loveseat—and eases himself into
it. He nods and smiles in her direction, throwing a civil crumb to the
enormity of her nervous expectancy. For the moment it is just the two of
them. It is not thunderously unbearable, the silence between John and
Mrs. Childress, perhaps because far too much is going on in it. Some of
these things are: her immense and genuine relief at John's appearing to be
whole, if not perfect; his awareness of the nature of her powerfully evident
concern, and sensing how removed it is from any financial matters; his
determination to present himself as coolly detached, and the weakening of
that intent under the current of her kindness; and his seeing that the first
thing she actually looked at was the walking stick. A Merlin's staff, the
stick changes things in the room. Silence will not, after all, do.

John is not cruel, nor even bereft of decency. He has in fact spent his
life in wishing there were more occasions deserving of it. He holds the
walking stick up; the eyes of Mrs. Childress grow, like those of a child
watching a magic trick.

"Thank you," he says. Anything more would be superfluous, would
diminish the simple and sparse dignity of the expression.

"*Oh*. You're so welcome. The least I could do…" Mrs. Childress turns
her head away and John fears that she may be crying. But she isn't. She is
modestly smiling, like a flirtatious girl, and John has an impression of how
petitely captivating she may well have been in her youth. A moment later
she faces him again. What they next say is draped in that richness present
when ordinary conversation is upheld, borne aloft, by a fantastic history
shared by its participants.

"Did you know, it belonged to my husband?"

"Really? It's very beautiful."

And that was all. John toys with the idea of asking her about the mysterious face carved into the cane's knob, but does not. Neither says anything more. It is something to remark upon, that this brief exchange would remain for each of them an inestimably valuable moment. Maybe she was a woman who loved gems and stumbled upon a great diamond, and maybe he was a toolmaker who needed the hardest substance known to man and tripped across the same stone. To each it is treasure.

Then the door opens like a cardboard one in a stage farce. Lawyer Duffy, Pepper from the insurance agency, and Mr. Cassius Sweet stride in. Tweedle-Dee and company, with an extra Dum. Duffy and Pepper carry furled papers like riding crops, lightly tapping their thighs with them as they shake hands all around. Then all five are seated, and the business of employing currency as a poultice is undertaken.

The entire affair is easy. John reflects that all the phone calls, all the delays, come to this, and he is stunned by the idea that there was a method to the maddening process. That they could sit for a few minutes in a ridiculous room, pass around pens and scratch out signatures, and resume life. Yet it appears that this is to be.

There is one point at which everything is momentarily halted; it occurs when Pepper, in a last ditch attempt to ease his employer's pecuniary burden, opines that the figure awaiting confirmation by all present is, really is, well, large. He does not say 'generous', for he has learned in insurance bars that the word conveys submission on the part of the giver. But 'large' is all right, and 'large' is what the sum is, and 'large' he calls it.

The room is devoid of sound at this. Then: Mrs. Childress shoots a look combining severe disapproval with watchful confidence at Duffy; who accepts the look and transfers it as one imparting a veneer of dull surprise over absolute authority to Mr. Pepper; and Cassius Sweet speaks. He says, "My client will never walk right, sir."

It is disagreeable to be spoken of in the third person, when one is in reality there. No matter what is being said, eulogy is in the air. Yet John is not uncomfortable at being so conversationally consigned elsewhere. He is too busy probing Mr. Sweet's pronouncement, which strikes his ears as less of a diagnosis and more of a curse. As though Sweet were in fact offering up something he could arrange, in return for so ample a payment.

Then the door opens again. Miss Marchbanks brings in a tray, sets it down on a fragile table by Sweet, smiles idiotically at everyone, and exits gracelessly. There is a doily over the tray's contents. Mr. Sweet delicately removes it, and says, "There she goes again." As John from his seat cannot see what lies on the tray–the bulk of Duffy's torso obscures it for him–his imagination is given yet another chance to run rampant. What is on the tray? Cookies, or paperclips? Finger sandwiches or cosmetic samples? John is inclined to suppose paperclips.

Mr. Sweet waves the tray before his guests with one hand. On it are what look like brownies. "Who's game?" he inquires. Mrs. Childress demurs with a barely perceptible shake of her head, Mr. Pepper stares into space at his lost opportunity of bringing down the settlement, and Lawyer Duffy puts forth a restrained guffaw and slaps a hand over his abdomen. John declines as well, knowing how easily cleansing powder may be mistaken for confectioner's sugar, even in the kitchens of the non-moronic.

As the unmolested tray is set down by Sweet, so too is Pepper's weak essay at a reduction of the dollar amount dismissed. The final sum is nodded over by all concerned. John spots what he sees as apprehension in Mrs. Childress' eyes and is sure that it is born solely from her desire that the money be sufficient to John. He meets her gaze and thusly tells her what she needs to know. Everything that has passed between himself and her in this room has oddly been elsewhere; this final intercourse punctuates the apartness.

Everyone rises and more hands are shaken. John would like to calculate the number of these handshakes made amongst so few people and in so brief a passage of time, but contents himself in knowing it is a disproportionately high number. Everyone rises and begins to file out of the flowery room. Lawyer Duffy will escort Ruth Childress, as is right. Yet she turns to see John's face one last time, and her countenance is that of a girl leaving the dance with the wrong fellow. Cassius Sweet startles John with a too forceful slap on the back. Mr. Pepper is solo and desirous of shortly finding an empty stool at an insurance bar. The world, he thinks, is especially unkind to insurance agencies.

Upon exiting, John finds he must squeeze past Miss Marchbanks. What she is doing outside this door is unclear but, as an entire orchestra of off-time percussionists seem to provide the beat this lady moves to, of no real urgency. She smiles widely at each of Mr. Sweet's departing guests. As John is the last, he is the one privileged to see the shock and hurt on her face, her mouth a bewildered 'O', upon spying the completely intact tray of brownies, or brown squares of cleansing powder.

Thirteen

Bucolic, and Illustrative of the Happiness to be Seen in Pairs

John and Rene are spending an hour in the park. She is profoundly and quietly pleased; he is enjoying the time with her, in between negotiating safe passage for them and awaiting someone's unmasking of himself as an imposter to life.

A squirrel gnawing on a chunk of hard donut is staring at them, as if considering an anthropomorphic and Disney-esque sharing of its bounty. The sun is downright mischievous; like a sorcerer madly delighted to discover real wizardry at his disposal, it vanishes and reappears in a million little places, everywhere. The stream babbles. If there is another word for it, it is nowhere near as good. The scene is purely and pastorally idyllic, anchored against the strong breeze by the ballast of two people thick with dimension.

This late morning in April of 1997 is to Rene evidence that bits and pieces of happy chance may sometimes occur in real life. She had been packing a coffee filter with sufficient grounds for a normal day's brewing when John had emerged from the little office of Garamond's and said, strangely softly, that they were shutting down for the day. That it was clearly too damn magnificent out to stay in, and that conducting business on such a day was maybe not a sin, but had to be recklessly wasteful. Only Rene and Reggie, the cook, were present to hear this declaration. Rene was cautiously stunned. Reggie's eyes narrowed to slits of suspicion at the news.

"Everyone'll get paid for today. Ren, I'll make up the tips for you", John had said.

Reggie's eyes assumed their usual parameters. Rene shook her head at the mention of her forfeited gratuities. John shook his head by way of reply to this. He would brook no argument.

"What about Andrea?" Rene lost no time, even at the zenith of personal delivery, in considering a fellow employee as yet not in attendance. Even a fellow without whom the rest of the lifeboat would be quite content to shove off. John informed her that Andrea had in fact just called in sick; that this illness had not even been minimally simulated by the girl, over the telephone; and that, rather than rage to the heavens, curse the day he handed the girl a checkpad and kick a wall with his good leg, he, John, had decided to extend the ploy to encompass all of them.

Rene turned to smile at Reggie. Nothing was there but an apron thrown over the pick-up window ledge.

*

Ten minutes after the elegantly handscripted sign announcing the day's closing is taped to the restaurant door, John and Rene are in Krutch Park. Tiny Krutch Park, in the center of the downtown. It glistens with dew and seduces with green. It is a moist diadem, an organic emerald, set square in the center of a pavement block. And, between noon and one o'clock on a fine spring day, it is a dry party much of Knoxville graces with a call.

His walking stick in one hand, John delicately cups the elbow of Rene with his other, slowly steering her to the bench across from the stream and the sundial. Their youth renders the careful progress of the short walk a sweet mockery of age. He is smiling; Rene can see this peripherally and does not want to break the spell by looking directly at his face.

"I should have put her on hold and told you to pick up the extension," he says. John is speaking of his earlier conversation with the delinquent and plainly healthy Andrea. "Just so you could've heard the pause. She was really expecting to be told to stay home for good. For forever."

"And instead, you said…?"

"I said, 'Sick, eh? Bad day to be sick, it's so beautiful out.' Then there was another pause, and I'd swear she was planning on dredging up some serious coughing. I *know* I heard keys jingling. And I said, 'In fact, it's too nice to be here. Think I'll send everybody home. Myself, too.'"

A younger couple passes them. They too walk slowly, but the pace is born of slovenly carriage, of indolence. The orange tee shirt of the boy is hard put to conceal the protuberance of his belly, which appears to be jutting out in pride, as chins sometimes do. His thin arm is around the naked midsection of the girl. As her jeans are barely and flimsily upheld by means of neither belt nor hip, this is quite a lot of territory, if of a predominantly vertical kind.

The pair's presence is, if not monstrous, utterly wrong. It is like a convenience store appearing in a pre-evacuated Eden. John does not intend it, but his eyes meet with the boy's for a moment. It is impossible to say within so fleeting an exchange who issues the unspoken challenge of contempt, for it is tacitly and immediately answered as it is so made. But it is indisputably there. The flash of recognition between natural enemies.

John and Rene sit, although not for long. With the passing by of the younger couple begins a bizarre pinball game. For the extent of their time in Krutch Park, John and Rene will ricochet off of similarly unappealing youths and bounce away from office people with nothing better to talk about than other men and women from other offices.

But, for the moment, they sit. Rene instinctively watches John's descent onto the bench, to see that it goes smoothly. It does. John's hands are then folded upon the head of his cane, propped before him. He makes himself smile; by staring directly ahead, he is even able to acceptably blot out the unsightly picture of the vulgar young couple. In a perfect world, in John's world, his thought alone would make them vanish.

Rene of course sees only John, John smiling broadly. The image bespeaks enormous self-satisfaction.

"You're very pleased with yourself, aren't you?"

"As a matter of fact, I am." But Rene's observation is as genial as the sound of the stream before them. Pettiness of any kind at all has no place in this day, this sunlight. And if John's sly turnabout on his devious employee had been even remotely tinged with malice, that too would have evanesced into harmless foolishness. Maybe four or five days in the course of a year are so empowered, that they can shame into nothingness all the little vices. Three are in spring; one or two, in the fall.

Rene's hands are folded modestly in her lap, and her head is a little down. The two do not speak for a few moments. It is not the inarticulateness of love responsible, but the silence is due to something equally grand and perhaps more lasting.

"Now, look at that." At John's instruction, Rene obediently shifts her gaze to the scene before her. She is about to ask what precisely should be commanding her attention. When she sees it. There is a small and strange tree some yards before them; it appears to have several trunks gracefully intertwined with themselves, like a Greek statue of wrestlers. Its branches overhang a portion of the running stream. And the sun reflected from the cascading water is not merely seen on the trunks and the branches, but runs ceaselessly over them. The effect is striking and curious, as though sunlight were visibly flowing *through* the tree.

From the gazebo the potbellied boy says, "Get the fuck outta here." The demand is clearly rhetorical, and poisons the immediate vicinity with foulness. The corrupting couple had not passed through the gates and exited the park, as John had hoped they would. It is amazing, he thinks, that the soil itself has not expelled them. He thinks, Oh, you are filth. He focuses more forcefully upon the tree and the light rippling over it. It is truly and uncommonly compelling. It should, it must, eradicate traces of nearby foulness. Then the hipless girl outright squeals with coarse joy in response to some playful maneuver on the part of her hulking companion. The sound is piercing and grotesque. Krutch Park itself recoils, seemingly ready to fold up its gorgeousness like an umbrella. The squirrel, still before them, scurries briskly away, as if to make quite clear that he is in no way associated with such people. John will in a matter of seconds echo both motion and motive.

First, though, he tries. He tries to categorize the girl's exclamation in his mind as a call made by an exotic bird. A stupid, inexpressibly crude, exotic bird. But the girl's rapture takes new flight and an "Oh, *shit!*" escapes from her, as another girl from another time would cry, 'My *dearest*'. Trying is absurd. John gallantly slips his hand once more under Rene's elbow. Orpheus to her Eurydice, he does not look behind them as he navigates their escape. A less inquisitive Eurydice, she too looks only ahead.

"Funny thing, apple again." John says this to both turn a bad page and mark their new stopping place: the little wooden bridge over the stream, a few short but mercifully adequate yards from their former point. He is refer-ring to the latest edition in the unsolicited subscription of Childress' pies.

"I know." Apple had made a second appearance. Both John and Rene were well aware that there are many sorts of apples and therefore many kinds of apple pies, but it seemed that this reprise of general content held something in the way of a message or inquiry within its crust. Strongly and disturbingly to John, and only strongly to Rene.

"Lemon meringue in March. But it was apple in…last year."

Her head demurely down, Rene says to the clear water below them, "Have you ever thanked her, John?"

"No."

"I didn't think so." There is sadness in this, but not dismissal, or hope-lessness.

"But not for the reasons anyone would think." Anyone but you, unsaid.

"No, I know," responds Rene. A great deal is conveyed by those few words to John. Not that she understands, but that she trusts in there being something, something substantial, to understand.

"Do you mind," he ventures, "if I try to explain a little?"

"You just better *not*!" This, not from Rene, but voiced gleefully by half of a duo suddenly visible from behind a cluster of shrubbery. As taken aback as both John and Rene are by the coincidental sentiment of the cry, it is more unsettling to identify the maker of it. Kelly Clifton-Cass. She had directed her warning to a pale young man in business attire accompanying her. Who was looking blatantly at her breasts, which were veiled in thin white cotton and, like spoiled children occasionally placed under a tissue of restrictions, unwilling to be disregarded.

Kelly and her transfixed beau stand on the grass by the little bridge, rather close to John and Rene. Whatever had prompted Kelly's exclamation was of course unknown to them; yet John felt secure in thinking, and muttering, that the young man would be disappointed if he expected further clarification to issue from the objects of his attention. Kelly quickly spots John and Rene. She calls out a greeting needlessly loud, given the small space between them, and even waves broadly. The gesture creates a chain reaction in Kelly's frame which in short order unleashes a tectonic burst of activity beneath her blouse. The young man turns his head to look up at the sun, for fear of going blind.

Once again John's hand deftly takes hold of Rene by the arm. Ricochet. Tilt. He escorts her onto the wide and serpentine path. Another bench is free and, for the moment, sullied only by those walking past. This can't be so bad.

Once again, they sit. Another tree is before them, a massive willow; somewhere within its boughs birds less peckish than the pigeons patrolling the ground are exchanging an harmonic array of messages. This, in fact, is lovely. It isn't as sublime as the tree with the sunlight running upon it, but circumstances dictate with no regard for the view.

"Here's the thing. It isn't that I don't want to thank her. I mean, in a strange, a really strange way, it's like she's my *benefactress*."

Rene nods in comprehension. Her hands repose in her lap again. She will take in what John has to say to the best of her ability, as she always does, believing that there is import in even his ordinary observations. As the topic at hand is in her mind perhaps the most pivotal on which she has ever heard him speak, she is doubly attentive.

"I have no reason to think it, but I have the feeling I'm not really supposed to thank her, or acknowledge the pies. Or even this." He lifts the walking stick like a baton and recalls the conference in the office of Mssrs. Gilley, French and Sweet. The understated gratitude he had then expressed to Mrs. Childress was born of the moment, not to be fought, but completely confined to that room, that minute. To explain it now, to Rene, would be to plunge too deeply into the waters in which the two now wade. "And, the more time that goes by, it seems more wrong to make contact with her."

Rene doesn't look at John during this, or even after, but at the willow trunk before them. Another squirrel, or possibly the same one, is poised on it, frozen. Rene's mind goes to an image of a daring thief scaling a tower and having second thoughts. Then she feels guilty for letting her mind stray, even for an instant, from what John was saying. Then she feels relieved, knowing on a yet truer level that her mind had been perfectly free to stray. He had said almost what she would have wished him to say, regarding the lack of communication with Mrs. Childress. He refrained from contact with the woman for reasons she didn't really understand, but there were reasons. As this was John, thought had gone into them. It was enough; it was fine.

At this moment Rene is gloriously proud to be in his company. John can't know this, but he can detect something better than what was there before. Coming from her.

The two rise in silent communion. Rene places her hand over his own, in turn cradling the knob of his cane. It may be the physical contact, the cliché of hands that has been responsible for what is quite literally the better part of all human history, that permeates John's being with a surge of raw happiness. Or it may be the birds and the grass and the water, and no one else intruding, too.

"You see this?" He raise his stick to show Rene the face carved upon it.

"No. Wow. That's…unusual."

John lowers the cane and looks away, dreamily smiling. "Yeah. Creepy, I thought at first. Now, it's something I like. Like a charm." Then he returns to the moment. He faces her and says, "Shouldn't we eat?" Rene smiles. Each turns a head in a different direction; she to the north, to Market Square, and he straight ahead, to see beyond the bank concealing Gay Street. But she plays guide on this last leg of their journey today, and takes a step to the north. He complies.

The north gates of Krutch Park lie before them. Behind them is the refuse of life John sneers at daily and spites whenever possible, the little miseries of humankind sullying an otherwise Halcyon landscape. Behind them as well, as new and exciting as a still-wet fresco, is the greater degree of their friendship, attained through his barely revelatory confession and her far greater depth of understanding. John will recall all of it; Rene, only what she deems worth remembering.

A few steps more, and they must settle on a restaurant. They will comment upon the rarity of the dilemma, both always supplying the service they seek this one stolen afternoon. There is the gate. Crowning three thin spikes of it are that many overturned and thusly empty bottles. As certain bottles swallow miniature ships, this trio seems to have a more ambitious design, and would engulf the entire fence. But that is for dreams of bottles, and in reality only a single and small spear tip is contained in each. And the thing he notices immediately is that the bottles could not have been randomly impaled. Not only was the litter of an evidently deliberate kind, but each of the three hung two tines apart from its brother. Someone took some primitive pleasure in this urban redecorating, and in so doing quite literally capped off John's internal summation of humanity that day.

*

That when two people are within one another's company for any period of time presupposes various degrees of misunderstanding. When the two people are Rene Dacres and John Grigio, the failures to fully comprehend the other are merely setbacks in the progress of more intimate knowledge. The communication between them is founded on excellent ground; when each goes a little wrong, the road is still a good road to take.

When the two people are Andrea and Rodney, the situation is so conducted on contrary levels that it is more mathematical than human.

That evening, the blonde and stalwart Rodney is sitting across from the diabolical circuitry of Andrea. They occupy a booth at the Sunspot restaurant, on the campus strip. The place is not fancy but, for this sort of tryst, any arena would suffice. A cafe, a circus, a laboratory.

"God," announces Andrea, "I can't believe how *hungry* I am!" She looks up from the menu and smiles maniacally at her companion. Whose left leg twitches, as though a knowledge within the marrow of the bone of that limb desires to communicate an urgent message to the rest of his system, advising one very big twitch out of the seat and through the door.

"Me, too," he replies, nodding lightly. Rodney nods a good deal in the company of Andrea, company he is enjoying for the eighth time as her escort. That this octonary occasion envelopes him now is something of a mystery, as neither it nor its preceding episodes were engineered, or even remotely premeditated, by him. He has tried to think of the why of these dates, but no answer comes. Instead, he twitches.

"So, what's going on with your job?" She makes this inquiry in an almost disgraceful aping of a caring interest, her face thrust forward, her skinny arms holding each other on the table top.

"Oh, nothing much. Not very exciting, really." To this, Andrea nods excitedly, suggesting fascinating depths within his reply and her eagerness to explore them. So, motivated by good guy decency and a fractional element of something that has to be classified as fear, Rodney offers up details of proposals made by Titch and Pratt and carried by him through the streets of Knoxville. One in fact involves a property near to the restaurant in which this enchanting hour is being passed; it is hoped by him that this coincidence will impart to his dull recitation, maybe, the tiniest reason for its being delivered. If not to her, then, please God, to him.

Because this entire affair of his seeing Andrea is incalculable. He does not exactly hate her, but a thorough autopsy of his emotional being would uncover not the most infinitesimal evidence of liking her. That he implacably does not like her is not so much a truth Rodney feels when in her presence; rather, it is one that steals upon him at odd times. As a young man is sometimes thunderstruck with the sudden and irrefutable knowledge that he is hopelessly in love with the girl not then actually with him, so does Rodney awake in the night, or stop at a red light, with a personal epiphany of nothingness. He has dated this girl, he is dating her now, and there is no single reason known to heaven or earth for it.

The trouble, naturally, is that Rodney achieves this perfect awareness when solitary. He is even prepared to act on it and—decently—put an end to this existentially bleak relationship the very next time she calls. But there is in Andrea a power that dampens his senses and extinguishes his resolve. On the phone, it disorients him just enough to ensure another meeting. Then, when in full physical vigor, it takes out his neural system. He goes along, inert, swept on the tide of Andrea's will.

"Uh-huh..." She yawns. She actually and expansively yawns, even while yet maintaining the posture of the transfixed. When the girl serving them stops by to take their order, she may as well be winged and haloed, so desperately is the respite needed.

"My job," Andrea contributes, "sucks." She chooses not to amplify this career summation. Rodney nods. Andrea has hated these nods since Rodney first bobbed his head thusly at the counter in Garamond's.

Which begs the question: why does *she* persist, not in keeping alive the relationship, but in strapping the two of them to this corpse? It is Andrea who makes the contact, each time. It is Andrea who cunningly manipulated the boy into first complying with her lightly made suggestion—as lightly made as steel is heated and molded into beams—that they would enjoy a drink together, sometime, somewhere. As it is Andrea who is having no better a time than her victim, socially or romantically speaking.

The answer lies within, not surprisingly, the entire Andrea. She is a fabulous machine. The pathological lying she employs as other people do polite conversation is merely a bell or whistle on the stunning apparatus of her. If people are bothersome and perpetually disappointing to a John Grigio, they are nonetheless people. To Andrea, they are stuff. They are oil to her gears, chips to her motherboard. She needs them badly, but is incapable of taking in any single facet of the few worthwhile qualities people may possess. This is not to say that quality in humankind is invisible to an Andrea, or Andreae in general; it acts in fact as a beacon, lighting the way to the best fodder out there. Thus is Rene viewed by Andrea as a friend, because Rene's basic goodness is a storehouse of exploitable scenarios.

Rodney orders a dish of chicken and oranges. His composure never flags, even as under his clothing the twitching erupts in his other leg, then moves to an elbow. He has enough experience of Andrea to know that this is the time when she will begin a deviant monologue and hold forth on her unreasonable roommate Kim, her childhood and, most frequently, her virtues as confirmed by her histories with people who ought to know. He could be a waxen effigy of Rodney, so inconsequential is his living presence then. Both Andrea's oration with herself as subject and the dampening field she rigs around him do not in reality transform him to wax, but his freckles become more prominent as his skin pales.

"You won't believe it, but she says I never gave her the money for the KUB bill. Do you *believe* that?" Kim is given especially lengthy verbal attention from Andrea this evening. Who had not liked at all the brief look she saw pass between the two when he had fetched her earlier. It wasn't love, or lust. It was worse. It was mutual commiseration.

Rodney says, "Wow."

Why does Andrea require Rodney? Because many other young women, including her nasty and larcenous roommate, would want him; because he was not in any way interested in her, but in fact sought her employer; because his blonde head is one to occupy pride-of-place mounted on her not fully sane walls; and because she wants to be able to say at future times that a great-looking blonde guy was in love with her, and because even she needs the barest props of him and these outings as a foundation for the untruth.

They eat. Andrea is reminded by her trashing of Kim of someone from her past, equally shifty of character. Rodney hears her and watches her eat, and suddenly has a vision of himself an hour hence, entering Andrea's bedroom. This accurate precognition sparks in his dulled brain the word, 'sacrifice'. As in 'human'. His right hand jerks.

As they prepare to depart the restaurant, Andrea makes, for her, an ordinary comment regarding the crowded waiter station near to their table, and draws a parallel between it and the cramped register space at Garamond's. This reference does not free Rodney–breezes do not as a rule break open shackles–but it clears his brow for a moment.

"How's John doing?" he asks.

Andrea says, "OK", something hydraulic hurtles something else up the length of her, a buzzer sounds, and she decides at that second that Rodney will make love to her twice that evening.

FOURTEEN

HOUSEHOLD GODS; A PEACH PIE; AND RENE'S STATE OF MIND

Spite Hall looks like almost any other small house, perhaps only more charming to those who prefer old red brick and broken flagstone paths. Nothing about its exterior suggests spite, and its indisputably modest dimensions belie anything hallish. Moreover, the stately and sinister name is unknown to everyone save its new owner, John Grigio. The mailman does not deliver correspondence so addressed, nor does the local gentry—of which there is none—overhear a lost stranger and obligingly provide the quaint direction: Ah, is it Spite Hall you're seeking? You'll find the old place where Gibb meets Fifth, and neither Gibb nor Fifth goes anywhere further. Tread careful, stranger.

Why this name no one knows, nor will ever know?

Almost every woman has in her closet a dress she never wears, bought because it suits an image of herself perfect in her mind and scandalously unacceptable to the world. Almost every man has one necktie of a hue or design he thinks very dashing around his throat, no matter that no corroborative appreciation has ever been put forth by anyone else. These are the conceits of our most crucial selves, the small grandeurs we cling to, the little vanities of the great icebergs of self. They are indispensable if we are not to utterly dissolve. For the world today likes nothing so much as to trumpet how modern life and technologies exist to confirm our individuality, while all the time strapping the same busy and awfully smart harness on all the individuals assembled in the same room, who gathered to learn better how to more fully mirror the individuals elbowing their sides. Yet the dress stays in the closet, and the tie occasionally gets knotted, and we hold onto who we think we are. May God preserve poorly chosen gowns and hideous ties.

John, as may be safely surmised, resists wearing or seeing or listening to anything large amounts of people tend to desire. The concert may be a fine one, but it must be nothing short of spectacular to be attended by him. For depositing himself in any midst is more disagreeable to John than illness. Does he fear people? No. He just does not care for them, generally speaking.

This antipathy to humanity in bulk form translates, not unexpectedly, to all that which draws forth the salivating tongue of bulk humanity. The technology of our time evolves so rapidly as to whiplash our poor necks; as John sees it, it is too good for the creatures who were stretched to their intellectual limit before it, resoundingly don't need it, and breathlessly buy it. Even the most harmless adoption of the most genuinely useful or attractive article is exceedingly hard for him, if said item is a hot property. When men turn to coats with four buttons, he searches in the back for their unfashionable predecessors. When a movie premieres to crowds composed of numbers higher than any census ever recorded as actually living in the city, he stays away. Does he fear an incompetence of self to keep abreast of all fashions and trends? No. He just refuses to care for the things people care for, generally speaking.

So, making no concessions to the herd, he has no reason to lovingly conceal his essence. He doesn't wear neckties that look stupid on him; he is too sartorially sensible for that. So John can have a whole house as his conceit. Spite Hall is his ugly tie, his shocking dress.

Thus we can safely expect to see in Spite Hall many a bizarre painting, several ugly if interestingly conceived chairs, a wallpaper in a pattern never before pasted to any walls and one probably designed to drive the intruding guest mad. But we don't. We go from room to room, anticipating misanthropic ceramics of happy harpies skewering less cheery victims, scanning for art which captures in primary colors the black pith of what is man. But we don't. We surely will not see a television set. But we do. For all Spite Hall is, as filled by John, is an homage to the world very young John viewed in black and white through another, older television screen. Subtly done, of course. It is a décor of ambiance and background, not a fan's display of sentimental iconography. Nothing on the walls or on a single shelf brings to mind, *per se*, the movies. Yet all of it, every small room, is arranged to be in perpetual readiness for a shoot. There are no magazines or stray paraphernalia that could not fit nicely in with a homogenized idea of simple and tasteful living quarters. The prints on the walls do call for attention; strangely, they are mostly portraiture of a past time, and one does not think to come across depictions of faces in the home of someone reclusive. But they are reassuring all around, those faces. They provide the sense of presence, albeit one-dimensional, the house of a solitary needs. And, as they are forever mute and denied the power to irritate through movement, they please John.

Visitor to Spite Hall: let not the name mislead you. Remember that the essence of spite is expansive, when physically demonstrated. That is, it reaches out to slap, it hurls or whispers a foul opinion, it pinches, and it sometimes does things behind backs. But all of it is a reaching out. It may not be the tenderly vulnerable sort of reaching out we are taught to look for and sometimes like to see, but an extension it certainly is. There is no reason to suppose that spite doesn't enjoy a warm fire and handsome drapes as much as the next fellow.

By late April, when the furnishings were in, the interestingly archaic pictures were hung, the pots were stacked like Chinese boxes in the cupboard and the shades were drawn against the outside, only one thing more was needed. Actually, the thing wasn't needed until the thing presented itself to John. Just as all those shiny items he despises are purchased by people ignorant of their need for them until better educated. New homeowners receive libraries of catalogues, the prevalent thinking in marketing circles being that big debt likes little debt scurrying below its feet. In one such catalogue John saw what he was missing for his new home. A gargoyle.

Gargoyles as such had never held a strong appeal to him. It is perhaps singular that they attract as many as they do, and stand sentry in so many otherwise not horrific flowerbeds. It's all very well to learn that the intent behind their medieval origin was one of protection against malign spirits of even more disagreeable aspect. But ugly is ugly, and John did not care for ugly. Yet he looked hard at a small specimen of the plaster breed. This, he felt, was right for him. The naming of his home was confined to his own mind, and was double-edged; the house had been obtained indirectly through spite, and spite was, if not his faith or credo, a thing he instinctively valued. And what in appearance could more resemble the nature of that reactive emotion, but a gargoyle? A gargoyle was the mascot of spite. He would have one. Within an hour of its arrival it was attached securely and affectionately just to the right of the ledge above his front door.

Visitor to Spite Hall: you know now that simple comfort lies within its unassuming dimensions. But do not let the name escape you.

*

The last pie came, not to Garamond's, but to Spite Hall itself.

Strange, that the address in which it was received should have made so great a difference to John. But it did. The homey nature of the gift was immeasurably amplified, handed to him by the man who delivered his personal mail. The unassailable goodness that is contained within the world of the pie, taken at the threshold of the home, was triumphant, invincible.

John carried the box into his kitchen and literally gulped on the way. It was an esophagal spasm of remorse, and he could indulge it because no one was there. Yet he had never before had to fight off such a sign of second thoughts; no pie prior to this had triggered in him much of anything beyond a dull acceptance. Was this new and oddly emotional reaction due to, again, the unheralded place of deposit? Because, for the first time, he was alone with it from its arrival? Or was it cumulatory, the pie that would break the cynic's back?

No. John set the box on the counter by the sink, set aside his stick and pulled himself up to sit, like a child in a nursery rhyme, beside it. He lit a cigarette and sat there, aware of the thing but not looking at it. August 10th. Summer continued to wind its heavy mass around Spite Hall, pushing its way into windows and patrolling heavily through each room. The gauze curtains at the kitchen window above the sink stirred only rarely, and with little heart. Flicking an ash into the sink basin, John had an abrupt and correct presentiment; this pie would be the last. He felt unaccountably sad at this.

He carefully slid off of the counter. He opened the cutlery drawer, removed a knife and cut into the box. If this was to be the last pie, as he was sure it was, he was seized with a curiosity as to its content. Already the fragrance of it had teased his senses. This pie brought forth in him the eagerness all of them should have prompted, the happy anticipation. This one, he thought, he would eat.

Peach. Well, of course. It was summer. Oh, but this pie was something extraordinary. This pie was loaded with power, as well as peach. That it had taken a different route to John than its varied cousins lent it mysterious, if not fully sensate, weight. That it was to be the final such gift, as John intuited, made it nearly sacred.

He cut a sliver, or as sliver-like a segment as the fat fruit would allow him to, and tasted it. It was the best pie he had ever tasted and John, the string of untried Childress pies notwithstanding, was very fond of pie. He then thought he would carve out a hefty slice, to eat in comfort while sitting in the living room. But he didn't. He simply stood at the counter, his good legs supporting his mass in the heron-like posture he had come to adopt whenever standing, and ate the pie right out of the box. He had consumed about one-third of it when he became aware that there were tears in his eyes. He had two or three more bites before he wrapped up what was left. He wiped the counter with a dish towel and unthinkingly used it to blot the tears now on his cheeks. And the more he realized that his crying wasn't an appreciative reaction to the excellence of the pie, the more labored his breathing became.

An hour later found John stretched out on his sofa. Sleeping.

*

It is not difficult to know when Rene is unhappy, or distracted. This knowledge is even readily available to those not intimate with her. Dissembling is not a thing she does well on those rare occasions when she weakly attempts it. And she never tries to disguise anything unless there is a very good reason to do so.

August, still. John is at the cash register, unsuccessfully inserting receipt tape onto the little spike designed to roll it, like a rotisserie chicken. Rene is at his side, a few feet away, beginning to make the day's iced tea supply. And all it takes for him to know that something is amiss with her is the way she is pouring the tea into the filter. With painful slowness, and a fixed stare seriously at odds with the fascination inherent in instant tea.

"You OK?" he asks. Then, "*Ow.* Son of a bitch." He has speared his finger tip on the little spike.

Rene turns to him, sees the trouble, and says, "I'll do that." Yet her eyes are, as when upon the tea, not there.

"Screw it," he managerially commands, then asks again. "Are you all right, Rene?"

She smiles. "Me? You're the one who's bleeding."

He smiles in return. "This? Kid stuff. Buicks can't even take me out."

Rene brushes a bang from her forehead; this strikes John as surpassingly elegant. It can happen, and often does, that a girl's prettiness is presented anew when an expression not normally upon her is suddenly worn. She says, "I'll get a Band-Aid from the back."

A minute later finds the two of them side by side, at the small counter. He wags his freshly bandaged finger and says, "See? I'm not bleeding to death. Honest. So…what's wrong?"

The door is slapped open and Andrea marches in with Rodney behind her. It would be alarming to see the knotted end of a rope in her hand, with the greater length of it harnessed around the boy's torso. But not terribly surprising.

"You sit on down, sweetie. I'll be back in a minute." Andrea skips off to the ladies room, having amply clarified her purpose in stopping by on her day off. Which of course has far more to do with slinging a fresh kill onto the table than a trip to a powder room.

Rodney is fortunate in the witnesses to this shame of his. They each smile a little and nod a little at his face. Then turn away, because the kill is not quite dead and it is too painful to see. Rene prepares an iced tea and sets it before him. It is all she can do to meet his sad eyes, even for the moment necessitated by the gesture. The kindness of ignoring him having been settled upon by both herself and John, she returns in her mind to the pre-interrupted scene.

At this point, on this day in late summer, Rene no longer wonders at the closeness she feels toward John. Nor does she question that it is to some degree reciprocated by him. She is as yet unaware of the extent of his feeling, but what there is of it is, to her, hard won and utterly dependable.

"Alice Ann." She sighs, lightly. "My aunt. She's what's…wrong."

"Ah. Yes. Alice Ann." He makes a long, low growl in his throat.

Rene is only superficially insulted; she trusts that John's venom would never be directed to her, or to her own. She has in fact let it go, the two other times he has rolled his eyes and made animal noises upon the mention of the name. "John. Why do you do that?"

Coy, caught, John. "That?"

"That. The growl."

"I don't really know. She just seems larger than life. That figure, those eyes going everywhere…" He pauses. He cannot of course say that he is sure the woman dislikes him. To someone else, perhaps, if the circumstance warranted such a disclosure. But not to Rene. Who, he has lately realized, seems to gain more in appeal for him with each new instance of his need to isolate her in his thoughts, in every circumstance.

"I'm sorry." He says this quite frequently and means it very seldomly. He says it when strangers and himself vainly reach for the same door, and when he merely needs to skirt by inches a fellow walker. It is for the most part a completely empty reflex within him. When he says it to Rene, he almost always means it. For a reason connected to that, he doesn't say it to her much at all.

"She means well," Rene begins, then contorts her own features into a parody of shock. "God, did I say that?"

"Uh-huh."

"Well. She does, after all. She wants me to be happy."

John goes through the motions of preparing a mug of coffee for himself. He does not want coffee, but when happiness is introduced into a conversation, it is better that the hands be occupied; else too much attention is being paid by the listener. The weightiest subjects call for, not rapt concentration, but something like string to weave between the fingers.

He reaches for the cream in the small refrigerator cabinet. "I'm sure she does. Aren't you happy?"

As the wife of the oil baron joyfully passes through a field of derricks to salute the drillers from the frosted window of her limousine, Andrea bounces from the restroom to the counter, tugs on Rodney's rope, waves a farewell to John and Rene, and exits with her prey in tow. The two remaining in Garamond's seek and confirm each other's incontrovertible opinion of what they have just seen. Each would have liked to have tossed the young man a blade sharp enough to hack through the rope around his person, but a knife cannot be thrown without a hand out to receive. There is just then nothing they can do for the boy. They return to the former moment.

Aren't you happy?

Now, Rene is a different sort of young woman. She is to John blessedly intact, a whole composed of the elements essential for the making of a true human being, and more wonderfully bereft of the clumsy attachments protruding from the standard model. She has, as he sees her, no hooks or suction cups, the little devices for taking fastened securely on most torsos. And there are no spikes or abrasive instruments to be seen on her, those armaments of petty vengeance strapped for life to the rest of the world. Above all, Rene is constitutionally unable to play games. These absences are what John has come to know about her, and what has made him esteem her as he does.

The problem then being: what does he see when he looks beyond what isn't there? Or the problem is: can he? For Rene, secure in his regard and sensing why, is still human. She would like to know more. Unequipped by artifice and fundamentally selfless as she is, it required the cascade of veiled remarks by Alice Ann to actually bring forth this desire within her. Thus has Alice Ann triumphantly wrought a spark from night after night of damp kindling. Alice Ann and everybody else should be periodically re-educated as to fire. And the first lesson should be, that each camp is responsible for its own.

"Are you happy?" Rene does not reply and looks John steadily in the face. There is nothing of specific confrontation in her eyes. But a long look is filled with everything. She knows that she may be making him uncomfortable, yet she is, again, human. There is no way around this, no matter what it yields.

"I'm not *un*happy," she says, and in so saying yields herself.

FIFTEEN

FOUR CONGENIAL LADIES; TWO ACQUAINTANCES; AND RUTH, ALONE

September opens her doors, so moist with perspiration, so indistinguishable from the preceding month, that her name seems an alias.

At the apex of the Plaza Tower, not very far below the patriotically hued sign declaring the banking to be had at ground level, there is a tableau of old women lunching. Four women, neighbors and friends to one another for many years, exchanging old stories and new notions; each offering a taste of her excellent dish to the rest, and the rest always politely declining; no one remotely overstepping the boundaries of the others' well-known sensibilities, but each storing away important new data to take home, as they will uneaten fragments of their meals. Four elderly women, lunching. It is a crackling and sedentary ballet.

The women are Mrs. Johnson, Mrs. Ansley, Miss Duffy and Mrs. Childress. The setting is the main dining room of Club LeConte, and the lunch itself is a prelude to a game of bridge to be played down the hall, in the relatively petite seclusion of the club's Governors' Room. As LeConte permits only members or their guests to enjoy its views and taste its food, the table and the room for bridge have been reserved under the banner of

Lawyer Duffy. Who maintains his membership chiefly because it is the best setting in which he may meet the respectable man who can make his sister happy. Who is, as has been noted, not at all unhappy, but only and unspeakably unfulfilled, in an hourly sort of way.

Their food is served. Miss Duffy makes noises about the enormous proportions of the salad set before her. Her server jocularly reminds her that it is still just a salad, and therefore cannot be too daunting. Two of the other women laugh lightly, while Mrs. Ansley notes to herself, as she frequently does, the ignominy of old women perpetually addressed as children. She does not scowl at the server, but her lips are tightly compressed. While Louisa Duffy's myopic eyes seek the young man's own; he is a nice looking boy, perhaps in his mid-twenties. He has smiled at her and made a joke. He is of course dressed in a uniform. All of this, and no greens, is the nourishment Miss Duffy craves.

Mrs. Johnson surgically pries into a crab cake with her fork. "Well, this looks wonderful," she says. All four women are simultaneously in various stages of lunch triage, poking and prodding what they have ordered. When one commences eating, the others will follow, and the one in this gathering to customarily take the first bite is Mrs. Ansley. The other three gladly defer to her this tacit prerogative, as the prestige of it is more than compensated for, in their minds, by the sacrifice of her gentility.

"What is that?" Mrs. Childress softly inquires of Miss Duffy.

"Salmon. Oh, I *think* he said 'salmon'!" Miss Duffy is the fifty-nine year-old bachelor girl of the prim cartel. In the distinct hierarchy of senior womanhood, both her unmarried status and her comparative youth act in concert to deprive her of any real standing amongst her peers. This is a role to which she unfailingly lives up. Nor does she object; when the girls dine out, there is almost always a good chance that a bartender or waiter will provide a roost on which her attention and her dreams can alight.

Mrs. Ansley holds her own fork still and examines, eyes narrowed, the main attraction of Miss Duffy's plate. It will not be salmon until she so pronounces it. But that is of small consequence to Miss Duffy's digestion, happily busy before the verdict is reached. For twenty minutes the women talk about the curtains in Mrs. Ansley's living room. That she has decided upon raw linen drapes is not necessarily a cataclysmic event in the lives of herself and her friends. But women, especially older women, very often do discuss drapes. Sailors really do talk about the sea, and musicians cannot help but be verbally hip.

Then Mrs. Johnson says, with a fork of grilled chicken poised at her lips and a quizzical look directed at Ruth Childress, "I was thinking. Wasn't it just about a year ago, Ruth, that your trouble happened? Doesn't it seem like longer?"

Mrs. Childress attends seriously to the question. No one speaks, until she herself replies. "You know, it does." Mentally, she counts pies. They parade before her mind's eye like a slowly spinning rack in a diner. But the others know nothing of her culinary offerings to John Grigio, and for good reason. In moments of self-inflicted fear, Mrs. Childress imagines to herself what the geriatric righteousness of Mrs. Ansley would be, if she knew.

"Just about a year, I imagine. Though it seems like *so much* longer." Nor can Mrs. Childress tell her friends that the time has passed sluggishly because she remains, to that day, confused and apprehensive about the incident itself. And about the young man she inadvertently injured. She can never, for instance, reveal to them that, on this very day, she had timed her arrival to allow for a slow stroll in front of Garamond's.

"Everyone says the boy is queer." Mrs. Ansley slams this home in her deliberately brusque way, as she slaps aces down in bridge; almost to punish the table itself.

Mrs. Johnson, most mindful of the quartet of their responsibilities to decorum for a world absolutely ignorant of the effort and completely oblivious to the example, is the first to flutter and respond. "What a thing to say, Ellen."

Mrs. Ansley wants to enjoy this. She wants her unflagging devotion to her friend augmented by excessively damning remarks made about John Grigio.

"Queer, queer, queer. As a goose."

"Nonsense, darlin'. My Jeremy told me, he *knows*, that there's a romance between that boy and the waitress." May the elderly always receive an extra blessing, that they do not acknowledge the sexlessness of modern job descriptions.

This gives Mrs. Ansley exactly the edge she has anticipated. "Merle. My lord. I meant 'queer' as in 'queer in the *head*', dear." Eating is resumed, delicately, as though four as yet undisclosed bugs lay in wait between four lettuce folds.

Miss Duffy does not look up, but says: "Well, you all know what my brother has said on the subject."

"Maybe not so queer as all that, though," muses Mrs. Ansley. "All that money he got from you. Ruth." She does not say, 'tsk, tsk', but it would be better if she did. An unvoiced reprimand from the roof of the mouth resounds more than one uttered.

"My brother," continues Miss Duffy, who might as well add 'big' to the designation of the male Duffy, so girlish is her social dependence upon him and his place in town, "saw everything, if you remember." Then Miss Duffy drops her head a bit. For this Miss Duffy, so dutifully sisterly, shames the Miss Duffy who resents her brother's intrusion in her life. This is a schism nearly intrinsic to relationships involving one partner's submission to the other's loving interference. Kisses and icy glares are alternately sent across the gulf.

Ruth Childress remembers, all too well. She remembers Lawyer Duffy's roundabout recounting of the peculiarity of the accident, of the young man's seeming refusal to move out of the way. She remembers how she'd known, before he went to the pains of educating her, that that didn't matter, as far as the damages went. And she remembers knowing too that what Duffy told her would remain with her, an awful puzzle, for a very long time.

"We remember, dear. Of course we do. *That's* why I say the boy isn't right, why I said so right away." Mrs. Ansley wishes, and not for the first time, that her own perspicacity took rightful precedence in the familially devoted psyche of Miss Duffy. "Really. Who on earth doesn't move out of the way when they see a car coming?"

The question hangs in the air, unanswered because the answer doesn't belong at the same table with four nice ladies. Even when one of them has begun to believe she could frame the answer.

More comments go from place setting to place setting, all sympathetic to the financial and emotional losses sustained by Ruth in the past year. Who is grateful for the commiseration, but would be more grateful still if her friends would never bring the matter up.

The lunches are cleared. The server wheels to their table a dessert cart. Three of the women express outrage, as though a tumbrel of freshly severed heads had been displayed for the obtaining of their aristocratic approval. Some women hold onto desirable waistline dimensions as the eccentric search for alien spacecraft.. They will not ever see a twenty-four inch circumference, they once came very close, and they believe in it devoutly. But Louisa Duffy's immediate and wide-eyed attention leaves the boy no choice but to perform his pastry sales pitch. By the red velvet cake, he is acutely aware that she has not for a second examined any of his frosted offerings. By the time he closes with a description of an ice cream dessert exclusive to the club, he is sweating. He wheels the cart away from the table and from Louisa Duffy's blatant avarice as a medic rolls essential equipment into an emergency room.

The years have wrought a particular specificity to Miss Duffy's fantasy life; the gigolo she sometimes dreams of employing, or the escort she imagines escorting her no farther than from one room to another, are increasingly dressed in the garments of waiters. At least, when they come to her door.

Then the last napkins are brushed across the last pair of rouged and withered lips. Mrs. Ansley comes to a decision. She says nothing of it to her friends; it is in reality only barely formed in her consciousness. But Ruth is an old friend. Ruth is clearly still undergoing distress from that horrible day, and Mrs. Ansley believes–rightly–that the young man has

never attempted any sort of the civil communication which would ame-
liorate her friend's distress. She, Mrs. Ansley, would see to it. It should be
made clear that the noble purpose of Mrs. Ansley, as all such noble purposes are, was only diluted by the satisfaction she took in her resolve, and
not extinguished by it.

*

John opened his door to the late afternoon sun of September 22, 1997.
Opened his door to a friendly ghost from the recent past. Bob.
Handsome, conspiratorial Bob from the hospital. His former accomplice
in nicotine abuse.

There was only a fractional delay of recognition. "Bob", said John. He
smiled, and said again, "Bob?"

"Hey, there. How you doin'?" Bob smiled wide in return. What a very nice
surprise, what a thoughtful visit. That impression was indeed made on John's
exterior. But only as a footprint leaves its shape in the sand by the water's
edge. Not deeply, and destined for an exceedingly short life. Men, even nice
men, did not *visit* other men with whom they had a slight acquaintance.

What this was, was odd.

Bob stood there, his hands in his pockets. Then one hand slipped out
and pointed skyward. "I like your friend." The gargoyle. Well, fine. John
nodded in mild satisfaction, to acknowledge the approval. But that was
odd, too; no one should like the gargoyle. It wasn't there to be liked.
Somehow this struck John as akin to sycophantic praise for an ugly child.

"Come on in", invited John, aware as he did so that he was helping to
take the wrongness in. He was giving the wrongness substance. But the
cigarettes from the past demanded something more than a 'can I help
you?'. Even the smallest favors live on as question marks.

Bob sauntered in, both hands returned to pockets. As his back glided
past John, the situation was awfully clear, and just that quickly. Bob was
violating something, merely by appearing in this fashion, no matter the

nature of his errand. He belonged to the world of Baptist Hospital; at least, he belonged to the smaller sphere of it within John's own life. The contact they had shared was almost excitingly intimate, the connection that can exist through a single channel of sympathy and mutual view-point. But was also entirely dependent upon the circumstances in which it arose, as such connections invariably are. Bob was not supposed to stop by and pay a call. Bob was supposed to be a good memory, and stay there.

He sat, did Bob. He declined the offer of a drink. John moved to a chair across from him. He did not intend to take an adversarial stance, but it was as well to face head-on the disappointment surely inherent in this call.

The peace of the nearly suburban locale, the sweetness of the nearly fall air and the steadiness of the glow of the almost evening light all combined to invest John's home with an atmosphere of removal from the world at large. This should have then rendered both John and home vulnerable. But the effect was contrary; the little house was a castle. So John, as lord of it, could look his barely known guest in the handsome eye fearlessly. Even as he thought, All right, let's have it. Let's get on with yet another example of the horror of *people*.

Bob inquired as to John's health, with particular emphasis on his ability to walk. John in turn asked how the hospital was currently treating him, the reflexive implication of corporate disregard for fine young employees such as himself carried in tone, if not by word. But Bob had no complaints.

Small talk is a singular little creature. It is usually like the presence of a pet in someone's home. The cat or the puppy calls for comment; more, comment, no matter how vapid or uninspired, is demanded by nothing more than the fact of it. So comment is made, and is interestingly as despised by the pet owner as it is by the pet admirer. Then the visit ends or the talk moves into a tolerable realm of interest. Yet there are occasions when the small talk itself seems to have a life of its own, when perhaps the cat or the puppy is actually a subject not employed until a better subject can be hit upon. These are disturbing scenes, and they make the partici-pants feel old.

John fleetingly tried to conjure up his Baptist days as a sort of rock on which the two of them could safely stand for a while. This meant verbally recalling the nurses as more sensational than they in reality were. This was a ruse hard to sustain. John wasn't near to sweating *per se*, but the pauses between sentences were increasingly leaden. The two spoke in dependent clauses, and the clauses had nothing to depend upon. He was grateful when Bob reconsidered his earlier decision to forego refreshment and asked for a soda, or anything cold. John's rising to fetch it brought forth fresh concern from Bob as to his impaired motor skills.

In the kitchen, throwing ice into a tumbler, John saw as potentially interminable this visit. Which had lasted, thus far, seven minutes.

Then things changed. It seemed as though Bob had merely needed to rid the two of them of the social amenities obligatory to this type of meeting before relaxing into himself, and into the real purpose of his coming. Which revealed itself as nothing more than a personable desire for further acquaintance with his host. To this end Bob casually and comically referred, through an unexpectedly deft segue from his job at the hospital, to the softball team for which he pitched. He recounted a few sliding and unfairly called moments from games played over the summer and did so in a way, if not enthralling, just above the margin of passably engaging.

The fading sun casting warm shadow into the room, the almost religious quiet to be not heard in that half hour when afternoon lights the stove for the coming night, and a story about a cleat sinking into an enemy's arm, worked a minor spell. If Bob had some nefarious motive behind his visit, he had chosen the perfect and most seductive time for it. But John intuited no danger, no imposition, of any kind. Each passing minute relieved the anxiety born from the handsome young man's inexplicable arrival. Bob's authentically modest attention to John's related—and meager—experiences with playing fields confirmed the wholesome quality and innocent intent of the visit. John offered Bob another drink, and Bob happily accepted it. A full hour went by.

Before everything fell apart, as it had to:

There is in the deepest recesses of every misanthrope a heart of something extremely soft. No science has yet isolated it, but that is meaningless; black holes are taken only on faith and a fair amount of quantum, but wholly circumstantial, evidence. It is reasonable to suppose that the misanthrope, in the earliest stages of his disgust, secretes a resin which envelopes the core of hope with which he was born and hardens around it. The core is tiny and the resin adamantine. Yet it is there. It is ironic that, almost always, only the holder of it is aware of its presence. He is sometimes ashamed of it, even as sometimes, when completely solitary, he takes off his shirt to ensure that it is still there.

John, in speaking with Bob, was in essence watching a massive cloud overhead. It was ominously dark. All of his experience told him, insisted to him, that a downpour was imminent. So almost all of John waited for the torrent, while a very little of John stole glances at his watch and gauged the cloud's speed across the sky. Thinking, but not dare saying to the cynical bulk of himself, it may pass. It may just pass, and rain someplace else.

Then. Bob asked John about his new house. He asked about John's job, observed that making ends meet was an arduous task for just about anyone, and more directly inquired as to John's mortgage having been facilitated by a settlement from the accident.

A hideous idea jumped into the front of John's head. His pliable core, reactivated from long dormancy, sparked, and attempted to dislodge the idea. But the core was atrophied from lack of use, and sluggish. And the idea was not new, had been around for quite some time, and carried a sound remarkably like thunder.

John realized that evasion was pointless, and would only serve to exacerbate the foolishness about to drench him. So he plainly stated that Mrs. Childress' insurance had been more than ample in covering his expenses and in helping to secure his new home. Which had a gargoyle above the door, to which John was planning to add Gothic brethren.

A proverb in Latin from the days when people were more ready to acknowledge evil in their neighbors, when wariness was in the roster of virtues, translates, 'daggers foreseen smite less'. It can be presumed that the foreseeing need not be lengthy; a moment, a look in the right direction, is enough. Thus when Bob sat back in his chair, provocatively stretched his handsome legs and said, with an appalling degree of studied nonchalance, that he was currently hurting for money, John was prepared.

"First of all," he said to Bob's legs, "I'm not *gay*."

Bemusement, then shock, on the angles of Bob's face at this.

"Secondly—" But there was no secondly. "Why don't you just leave. Please."

This, Bob did. With no fuss at all. Even a part-time hustler has the full soul of a hustler, John reasoned, and hustler souls dislike more than anything the wasting of hustling time.

After he had departed with his carnal schemes, John sat for a while, indignation welling up within his chest. The audacity of the boy was almost admirable, he thought, if one could get past the reprehensible, chilly greed of it. That he had so flagrantly adopted a pose transparently intimating seduction, on John's own furniture, in John's own house–it was to John a vile version of the sort of boldness that burns in the hearts of great explorers. An element of his outrage was due, not inexplicably, to the boy's supposition that John would desire him. A sharper and more submerged factor in that outrage was the boy's counting upon, not merely the lust, but a willingness on the part of his host to pay for it. The presumption of retaining base urges is not a thing to enhance the prestige of a person so identified, but is not altogether disgraceful. Adding a bottom line to the equation, however, is nothing short of insupportable.

After a minute or two of dental gnashing, John stood and cautiously went to his front door. Some primal need to scout the territory possessed him. He opened the door, put only one foot out, and looked to the right and to the left. Then he turned his head to look upward. Anyone walking by would have seen, naturally, just that: a small granite figure designed to drive off the unwelcome and, just below it, a man echoing in living disgust the same purpose.

*

That evening. Ruth Childress sits in her parlor. Unrest is in the lightly perfumed air, as it has been for nearly a year.

Darwin Childress had died six years earlier. This she had borne with Christian fortitude, a stoicism that deeply impressed her friends and was far easier to maintain than any of them could have known. For Ruth had never loved Darwin. She had liked him, married him, lived with him contentedly, and missed him only as an absent friend upon his passing.

It is as well that no one in their circle knew of the lack of romantic feeling between the pair. Such things are too frequently misunderstood; people assume that a lack of burning love in a marriage points to a truer passion unfulfilled in one partner's past, or a resentment simmering over the years, or all sorts of melodramatic possibilities. People, she has observed, believe heartily in others enjoying the rich emotional life they very often do not themselves have. Too many movies, she has sometimes concluded.

Her small hand, more jewel than hand, is held at her mouth in a fist. She looks like a diminutive monarch, a petite Beatrice in Tennessean suburbia. She is worried that her friend Mrs. Ansley will do something. Everyone has at least one friend of whom he is slightly afraid, and Mrs. Ansley is Ruth's. She is too courageous for courage's sake, too ready to mount a charger when no one wants to go to war. Ruth is genuinely fond of Mrs. Ansley, and has wished for her whatever passion is missing, that would have rendered her feistiness unnecessary.

Ruth is thinking tonight of John Grigio, and of other things. She is thinking with something like shame of the pies she has baked and sent him, warm gifts that brought forth no response of any kind. In no way, however, does she regret having presented him with her late husband's cane. That was right, acknowledged or ignored. Then she recalls John's understated expression of gratitude for it. She holds onto that as some-thing important, as she has in other contemplative hours.

Thoughts enter, wander through and unceremoniously depart all minds, young and old. Tonight Ruth sees John in her mind, then Darwin Childress. He comes to her like a friendly talisman. All the years of peace with him, of the almost loving life achieved once no love was expected, is her anchor. Hundreds, thousands of evenings witnessing the small but brutal collisions of feeling between their married friends; how easy it was to solidify their shared conviction in having made, if not a glorious and exciting union, a perfectly all right one. No blood raced in either Childress, but neither did sarcasm ever fly in their home.

John is there, again. It is difficult for her to recall the accident. It has been, from the start. Because she has a hard time facing, each time, what she knows to be true, that he had stopped and stood in the middle of the street intentionally. She has never once thought that he was suicidal. She has met him only twice, both times in the offices of Gilley, Sweet and French, and had been taken each time by his old-fashioned demeanor and absolute correctness. He was never hostile, by word or by intonation, and quite correctly addressed only those representing her. She liked him.

The evening deepens. She decides to make a snack for herself, maybe watch a film on television. This plan excises her musing, and in fact cheers her. Thirty minutes later, a sandwich on her lap and the remote control in her tiny hand, she flicks on a station she relies upon to provide the sort of movies she likes best. She is in luck; a wonderful musical is just beginning. Seven men will romp and cavort as no seven woodsmen in reality ever have, to procure the affections of a coincidentally identical number of maidens. Just as she settles into the minor happiness before her, she has a powerful thought, based upon nothing but instinct: she and the young man are alike. She has a sense that John Grigio would like, or does love, this same silly movie, and that it would be rather nice to be watching it together. Maybe whatever Mrs. Ansley is planning, and God alone knows what it is, is for the best.

Sixteen

In Which Much of the Company Nears a Single Horizon

October in Knoxville. At no time in the history of man's sojourn on the planet, and in no place on it he has ever befouled with his presence, has there been more orange. Except in Knoxville, every other fall.

There are pumpkins here and there, on porch steps, on the ledges of the banks' teller windows, in unwholesome heaps on the sidewalks outside the supermarkets. Their orange is subdued and attractively earthy, in comparison to the greater display of it on Knoxvillian bodies. Caps and sweatshirts, windbreakers and headbands move through the streets in baby parades of team spirit. But even this much orange is insufficient orange, so the cars of the city are stuck with orange flags, orange posters are plastered on windows, and the word 'orange' is used incessantly to characterize the blood type of the town's inhabitants. If Newcastle had had this much coal, electricity would still be just an idea.

From eleven-thirty that morning, Mrs. Ansley has been sitting at the little table farthest from Garamond's door. It is now one-forty-five. Andrea has asked her twice if there is anything else she requires. There is not.

"Ren, do you mind if I go? Everything's done." At this, Rene's eyes sweep the tables and see the unfilled salt and pepper containers. "My checks are done, my tables, everything. Do you want me to stick around just to bus that last table?"

Rene's gaze now goes to Mrs. Ansley. She thinks, as she has thought several times in the past ninety minutes, that the woman has a specific reason for dallying there. "No," she tells Andrea. "You may as well go." Which Andrea does, with a conciliatory exhalation of weariness over the continued fact of the old woman in the corner.

That Mrs. Ansley's agenda pertains to John is clear to Rene as well. Every time that he had passed by her table, every time Rene had been in a position to take in the lunchtime dynamic of the room, she had seen Mrs. Ansley's eyes fixed upon John. Not hatefully, to be sure. But steadily. Like a not especially hungry bird of prey.

Ten minutes later John reappears from the safety of his tiny office. A seasoned restaurateur can, like a veteran actor, count the house without even a glance at any single part of it; John knows that the old lady is the only occupant. He will send Rene home. In fifteen minutes, if their guest remains immobile, he will politely tell her that they are shutting down for the day. He briefly thinks to himself: Oh, silly old women with nothing but time on their hands—why isn't she playing canasta somewhere with her tribe?

Then a long and slender hand gracefully rises from the corner. The fingers gently shake. John notices this and walks to Mrs. Ansley, hoping that the motion is indeed meant to catch his eye and is not palsy.

"Mr. Grigio?" Mrs. Ansley pronounces his name beautifully, making it sound foreign and elegant. This, combined with her natural air of authority and the sense of prestige she bears in performing this duty in her friend's behalf, creates something more than merely an imposing presence at the little table in Garamond's. Mrs. Ansley is downright ambassadorial.

She introduces herself and gestures for John to sit, having ascertained that he has a moment to spare her. The ketchup bottle on the table appears ridiculously out of place, as a prop in so courtly a tableau. John marginally wonders if a diplomatic pouch is cradled on her delicate lap. But he says, "I'm very glad to know you." John, again, had absorbed many old films in his youth. And if the movies of the thirties and forties gave us anything, they gave us a thousand such unimpeachable salutations.

Mrs. Ansley lightly slides her hand over John's on the table surface and says, "I'm a friend of Ruth Childress." She then winks at him. John is unsure if he is to hand over a packet of money or experience a blade plunged through the hand so gingerly held on the table. But something not in keeping with a ketchup bottle is surely expected. So he plays for time. He looks at Mrs. Ansley, and his features are set in the unfinished fashion faces are, when a more proper reaction must be manifested. As soon, that is, as the situation makes any sense at all.

"How are you *feeling*, dear?"

"Quite well, thank you." The more surreal the encounter, the more John dipped into his reservoir of grand phraseology.

As a sculptor will pace around a hunk of marble for hours, strike a single blow with his chisel and then retire to a cigar and a mistress, so too had Mrs. Ansley sat for over two hours, to deliver her stroke. "Here's what I was thinking, dear. I have known Ruth for many years. She is not herself. I suspect that anxiety from last year's unfortunate accident is responsible. So, Mr. Grigio, if you truly are 'quite well', I do think it would be the right thing for you to meet with her. May I depend upon it?"

Poor John, to have only a healthy supply of fancy phrases at the ready and to be confronted by a true practitioner of the art. He is an American in Rome with a Berlitz in his hand and a contessa across the table. He is, quite simply, stymied.

"Well. Ah…Mrs. Ansley, I appreciate what you're saying…"

But Mrs. Ansley is now risen. Her work is done.

"I took the liberty of telling Ruth that you'll be expecting her on Saturday. I do hope that's convenient." This, with a tough little tug at a stubborn handbag strap on her forearm. This woman, sees John, has hidden power. It is not a far reach to envision her tugging at anything which won't give. "I thought four would be a good time. Oh, and our Ruth is punctual."

Mrs. Ansley extends her hand. It occurs to John that the very brevity of her assault was calculated to incapacitate him, and he will give no one, even tough old ladies, that satisfaction. She has won the battle, but he'll be keeping his horse, thank you.

He stands and, in as chivalric a manner as he can summon without stepping into the ludicrous and clicking his heels, he takes the tips of her fingers in his own hand.

"Four o'clock, on Saturday. I'm sure that'll be fine."

Mrs. Ansley's brows arch in pleased appreciation. She leaves.

"Lock it up, would you, Rene?" John calls out to the counter.

"What was that about?"

After a moment, John answers, still at the table. "I'm having a mad tea party this Saturday. You free?"

*

On the Friday evening of that week, Andrea is making her last stand. This is something, for the pathologically untruthful. Shifting is their more natural comportment.

How long has she been dating Rodney? Quite a while. Their trysts have not been, however, particularly many. Weeks have passed between them, in fact, and this very broken sequence is highly symptomatic of what must be termed their relationship. It wants to die, it wants to die badly, no matter the intentions of one half of it and the numbing malaise of the other. Yet, just when it seems that the awful affair may breathe its last, depart from this life and end its wretched existence, Andrea kicks it around again. So it writhes, a miserable thing, but not yet dead.

But even Andrea is dissatisfied. Rodney is to fetch her for a date tonight. She is brushing her hair feverishly in preparation, like an apprentice Amazon ready to earn her bow and sheath. For she has had, by her estimation, quite enough. Rodney is a fine young man, an excellent specimen. She knows this as a coroner can clearly detect good muscle tone on the lifeless casualty before him. On their previous outings he has even expressed admiration for the physical charms she employs like a thug uses brass knuckles. He has acted upon these desires, too. Customarily in the history of Andrea these attentions are halted only by the permission to proceed she imperiously withholds. Rodney, however, has stopped short, and of his own accord.

And that's no good. That is a problem. A nicer girl, or certainly a saner one, might interpret his disinclination to stake further sexual territory as a sign of an exemplary character. This is not a possibility Andrea is remotely capable of conceiving. If suggested to her, she would laugh, not with derision, but with incomprehension. Andrea is not evil, as moray eels are not evil. It is more that each species knows nothing save its own world, and the meal swimming to the left. So Rodney is unacceptable, as is. He goes along and takes what she thrusts at him, but never wants more. That Andrea *has* no more to offer is not the point. He never seeks to take their relationship further, he never gives her the opportunity to crush him, and this has got to stop. Because under it all is the nagging possibility that Rodney knows exactly what she is. Thus, tonight, Rodney must demonstrate with no equivocation that he both buys into the Andrea machine and wishes to buy into it further. Or Rodney must be discarded, and the hyperboles she will eventually wrap around her reminiscences of this affair will have to be far fancier.

Incidentally: does Rodney truly know what she is? Not precisely, but few truly know what lies in each corner of their cellars, or moves below the floor.

Andrea slips on a white sweater with bands of orange running across it. She bears as much unflagging loyalty for the home team as she holds within her authentic interest and fondness for the young man soon to escort her. None at all. But she is brilliantly adept at going through motions. Going through motions well smoothes the way. Just where the way ends is not a consideration of Andrea, as long as her carriage sees her safely there.

Kim sits in the living room principally financed by herself. She thinks of that glorious moment of untruth, when Andrea had teased her with the possibility of her own vacating of the house. Nothing had come of it, just as money for bills was now inadequate as well as very late. Which was Andrea's nasty little spin on the kind attempt Kim had made in the kitchen months before, to educate her.

Kim is thinking about Rodney, and herself. She is thinking that, because of her femaleness, she was not snared by her in the same manner as she is sure Rodney was netted. Kim only and tragically took Andrea at face value, and understandably did not perceive all that lay behind the face. It was that simple, as it is with most of the people with whom Andrea is connected. Then began the string of lies revealed as such days later, the promises not kept and denied when referred to, and the general weary acceptance of what she, Kim, allowed to unpack down the hall. She has made several and unsuccessful stands against the sociopathic tyranny with which she dwells, but no longer. All indications are that she has caved, and unconditionally. And Andrea is accustomed to this pattern, albeit subconsciously. She has no cause to not anticipate Kim's eventual and total submission, her fate as more pulp in her path.

Surely Napoleon or somebody equally territorially rapacious learned to his cost that silence is not always surrender. Or: is Kim so completely resigned? Is there nothing she can do, perhaps through no means greater than her presence?

The clock moves forward. Kim is eating from a bag of chips. As the time of her roommate's date nears, there is a chilling sameness to be observed in Kim's consuming of the chips. She appears quintessentially late 50's at this moment, her shapely legs in Capri pants tucked beneath her, her brunette hair in its youthful ponytail, a glimmer of something perhaps wickedly not in keeping with a cold war *entente* in her brown eyes. She takes each chip out of the bag with the same slow hand, brings it to her lips at the precisely same unhurried rate, and parts her lips to receive it at exactly the same moment of equidistance of chip to mouth. If it appears to be a succession of communion wafers taken to expiate sin, the sin is relatively weak. It is one of loathing for her roommate, paired with disgust at her own folly for not having originally seen the creature for what she is.

A car horn blares from the street. Chip poised, suspended between thumb and forefinger, other digits daintily and eerily held aloft, Kim's eyes turn to the sound. She smiles slyly, doubly pleased that Rodney has chosen to call for his date in this adolescently barbaric fashion. It means–to Kim, at least–that she was right in sensing embarrassment on his part when he had been introduced to her on an earlier occasion. Good. And it means that the witch will have to exit past Kim, in all the unglory of being so unceremoniously called for. Oh, very good.

"G'night!" screeches Andrea, flying past her. "Have fun!"

This, Kim recognizes, is a tired weapon of the witch, unholstered to zing the dateless under the pretext of caring. As with Rodney's heart, Andrea could not ever know the reality; that Kim will indeed be having a sort of fun. She already is, stretching her arms above her head and musing over what she intuits to be, if not the undoing of the witch this night, a prelude to it. Or maybe just the slapping around of her.

*

The next day, and just a bit south of the last.

"Louisa. Dear. I don't think we're allowed to park here, you know."

Ruth Childress is perhaps more fretful as a passenger than she was awestruck as a driver. But there is nothing to be done; driving is too distressing to her these days, and she relies upon her circle of women friends for transportation. As her destinations almost always coincide with the meeting up of one or all of them, this is no imposition to the ladies. They must, as Mrs. Ansley aggressively reminds them, look after one another anyway.

Today, though, is a different sort of errand. Only Miss Duffy has been approached by Mrs. Childress for vehicular assistance. If that woman had been unable to comply, a taxi would have been summoned to meet the need. For Mrs. Ansley must not ever know of this undertaking, Mrs. Johnson would unfailingly report it to Mrs. Ansley, and Miss Duffy and cab drivers can be trusted to silence.

"Of course we can, Ruth," replies Miss Duffy, swinging her Cadillac into the Baptist Hospital emergency room parking area. Something is going on within the steely bulk of Miss Duffy; years of suppression are massing, passing around seditious handbills, inciting even the most submissive elements of her being into rebellion. She is feeling, these days, bolder. She jauntily slips the huge car through the parking attendant's pincers, rolls down her window and extends her hand.

"Is it all right, that we're parking for a bit?" This from Mrs. Childress, meekly leaning from the passenger side.

The attendant hears only an irrelevant question and not the words themselves. She may as well be asking him if there's a fire in the east wing.

"Sure thing, ma'am."

Why are they there? Simply because little Mrs. Childress wants to do her homework. If she is to get together with John Grigio, she wants to be knowledgeable about what she herself has caused. She wants to speak to the man who operated on John, so that she will at least know the truth of his situation, the real extent and expectations regarding his injury. She is ashamed for not having sought this information earlier. So Ruth called Louisa, and asked for her help.

The air crackles as the two women make their stately, yet choreographically incompatible, way into the building. It is the charge, the tangible current, of fall. Louisa Duffy finds it enormously enervating; she has not felt this good, this internally alive and expectant, in a long time. She has to work, to slow her brisk pace and keep up with her friend. If anyone didn't know better or if someone knew everything, Louisa walks to the sliding glass doors as though she cannot wait to enter that most dreaded of locales.

Inside, it occurs to each of them that the hospital is a rather sizeable establishment, and that they may be at the farthest point from where they seek to go. This is in fact confirmed by the receptionist; Dr. Perkey—Ruth knows the name by means of Duffy, and trusts the sound of it as one promising to gladly enlighten an ignorant old woman–is in the medical, and less emergent, tower itself. A block away.

"Oh. Dear."

But Mrs. Childress is reassured, this time from an actually attentive source, not only that she committed no crime in parking where she did, but that her target is perfectly accessible from within the fluorescent confines of the building itself.

"I *told* you, Ruth." Louisa Duffy delivers this traditional hand slap buoyantly, with not even a particle of condescension.

Something is happening within Miss Duffy, and it appears to be happening right then and there.

The two women move away from the counter and strategize, as it were. Foremost in Ruth's mind is that her friend not be incommoded through tedious waiting, so she mentions the coffee shop as, perhaps, the best place in which Louisa can comfortably pass the time. Mrs. Childress suggests the coffee shop tentatively and employs the word 'perhaps' because the crackle in the air outside is brisk autumn air to her, and nothing more. To Miss Duffy, the coffee shop is without question just the thing, and the ladies proceed accordingly. At the café's door, Louisa is nearly given a large diamond from the finger of Ruth, as token of her vow to return within a reasonable space of time. This consideration intrinsic in Ruth, habitually in evidence over just such minor arrangements, typically draws from Louisa mild and silent gratitude.

But not today, not at this moment.

For Louisa Duffy looks into the transparency of the coffee shop door and stares at her dream. 'Stare' is not a pretty word and 'gape' is less attractive, yet the further abasement of 'gape' is demanded, and so we see that 'gape' is what Louisa Duffy does. Her mouth opens and remains so, although breath makes no headway in, or exits thusly. Her eyes glaze in animal apogee. She sees Bob.

From a more cosmic perspective, Mrs. Childress' scurrying down multiple hallways to complete her kind and tidy mission is the movement of a timid mouse, as deep bass strains rumble below the Oxfords on Louisa Duffy's flat feet. The crackle permeating the outside air was nothing, really, but an augur to symphonic explosion. Miss Duffy's thought processes, seemingly shut down to accommodate the power demands of a sudden surge of a heretofore unguessed-at level of lust, are in actuality quite busy. They are closing a hundred files on goodlooking boys in waiter attire who, it now turns out, were nothing. They are noting the existence of dormant might within what had previously been categorized as weakness, a persistent and minor failing. And, rather proudly for such coldly functional devices, they are recognizing the remote but nonetheless extant possibility that the crackle was *of* Louisa, and not around her.

Before Miss Duffy swings wide the coffee shop door and marches to her dream: we would do well to remember that circumstances we may suppose largely foreseeable–say, the rebuffing of a plain and nearly elderly woman by a beautiful young man–conduct themselves and generally carry on with no regard for our assumptions. Sometimes, in fact, circumstances so pan out as to leave the most sanguine of us...gaping.

SEVENTEEN

HORIZON, LOOMING LARGER

The Saturday arrives, in gunmetal gray the shade of Miss Duffy's hair, and stillness.

John has not given any real thought as such to his impending guest. He has not speculated upon how the time will pass, what will be said, and what if any sentiments will be exchanged. From the moment Mrs. Ansley blew her heraldic trumpet and set the date, he made the conscious and correct decision to think about none of it. There had been, he considered, too much thinking already. Let her come. Whatever the content of the visit, it could not cripple him, and it could not last forever.

He does wish, however, that Mrs. Ansley had pencilled the two of them in a bit earlier. He is not good at delay. Time hung heavy on his soul when there was knowledge of anything to be faced later on in the day, and he typically occupied himself during such intervals with straightening pictures and smoking too much. However. Today, he has an inspiration of sorts. He will make an unnecessary trip to the supermarket and look for little things old ladies like to, if not eat, see presented to them.

So John pulls into the nicest Kroger in town, the one with the façade more befitting a cinema and subsequently stocked with more attractive offerings and a less fragrant clientele. He finds a parking space not very far from the doors, refusing as he usually does the convenience and distinction of the handicapped spots. He is ceaselessly as hard upon himself as he is to the rest of humanity; he can walk, after all. Below this stoicism is the more commonly exposed, John-like thought that: whoever does use the designated space just better be awfully hurt.

Today, even in aisle four, feels somehow climactic, in a moderate and pleasant sort of way. He suspects this feeling would be with him were there no Mrs. Childress to anticipate; as though, today, one could take a nap and wake up to a world noticeably more right. Or at least more intelligible.

Aisle five. His cane in one hand and a basket dangling from the other, he surveys canned goods, dismisses them as canned, and looks for small jars. Which normally contain better small things. Then his path is blocked by a trio consisting of a man, a cart and a woman, and only the cart would be exempt from the violent action John wishes he could use against this entire blockade. The couple is transgressing the most basic market etiquette by consulting over an item, side by side. As both parties have somewhat broad girths—the brother and sister act of couplehood, the bookending of physical dimension—the cart itself is hardpressed to maintain a straight-on stance between them.

An ordinary and slight impoliteness. Comedians frequently draw upon just such fodder. And yet another example of the discourtesy involving any kind of motion John finds utterly intolerable. He would like to strenuously tap the man's back with his stick, or use Ruth Childress' gift to pull the silly bow off the woman's head. Instead, he raps it upon the floor, wondering if the sound will penetrate into the obliviousness of such an oblivious pair.

The woman turns and smiles wanly. It is Miss Marchbanks. She does not identify John in her mind as someone she knows. For this, John is grateful. Her companion, the increasingly devoted suitor from Sir Speedy, turns his head as well. And shrugs. The shrug, more than the obstacle, more than the stupid bow in the hair of that idiot woman, creates within John's sternum a stabbing pain. A shrug is a fat cousin to a wink, when applied as a tacit and friendly affirmation of shared ignorance. It is a caveman's insufferable declaration of his pride in his purely mindless existence when shoulders are thusly jerked, as in the above scenario. As if to say, the culpability may rest upon the jar in my hand, on the width of the aisle, on the state of the union, but not, absolutely not, upon me.

Like a man pressing his way through a spellbound crowd to get to the injured relative on the sidewalk ahead, John pulls his basket to his chest and lurches between the hulking still life. Miss Marchbanks smiles, weakly still, at his back. She thinks she may have seen that cane before, but her brain does not associate that eventuality with its owner perhaps being known to her as well. The brain of Miss Marchbanks does not so much occupy another realm, as move to an exceedingly feeble metronome.

John brings his few purchases to the check-out line. In a manner of thinking that is not linear thought, he imagines smashing the front window of Miss Marchbank's car. It is likely that he would be identified as the perpetrator of the vandalistic and spiteful act, but that would be all right.

*

Randolph Duffy, Esq., is possessed of a minor inspiration today, as well. He will drive to his sister's apartment and treat her to lunch and, perhaps, a movie.

Winding through the largely inactive thoroughfares of West Knoxville on a Saturday morning, he ruminates on his sister and their relationship, as we strangely and unwittingly do an hour before the world explodes. The elder Duffys had passed on when both children were relatively young, and had decorously done so within a few months of each other. Randolph, already lush of eyebrow and steady in character in his late teens, took it upon himself to complete the rearing of Louisa. This was expected by everyone who knew the family; so ideal was young Randolph to assume the reins of parenting, in fact, that a cruel observer might have pointed to the mother and father's surviving as a shame, a waste of talent.

There has never been anything but kind intent and authentic love behind Randolph's every decision made on Louisa's behalf. Sometimes he has even taken the trouble to consult her as to her own inclinations; when, many years before, she had toyed with the idea of beginning some sort of career, he had dutifully listened and taken in as much of her meaning as was possible for him. The family's legacy, decently adequate if not embarrassingly gilded, made such a career unnecessary. Perhaps that alone accounted for Miss Duffy's inability to fix upon one. Perhaps it was that, along with her brother's reminders of it. That dividends from an ancient speculation in, of all things, a railroad would ensure the continuance of the modestly genteel Knoxvillian life they knew was a fact he brought forward repeatedly. Not to discourage, but to comfort.

He drives on, blameless. It is not his fault that we do not always know fully well what we love. He nears the apartment complex which houses his sister. It is nice enough, but rather fast, as he sees it. It is a mystery to him that his sister would choose to live amongst people far younger than herself.

He parks outside her townhouse. The entire complex is still in a disquieting way; the gray of the sky seems to fall over it, muting whatever life it contains. But, he reasons, it is Saturday. The inhabitants are most likely sleeping off indulgent behavior, or out purchasing electronics they cannot afford, as young people do.

He walks to her door. He is today as casual as the surviving male Duffy can ever be, in a recklessness of serge trouser and button-down shirt. As he takes the few paved steps he quickly experiences, not anxiety, but the small unease he felt upon last seeing Louisa. The meeting had been brief, in his office, and involved nothing more than an exchange of signatures. But Louisa had been different. He was unable to pinpoint in what this change lay at the time, nor has he been able to in the intervening days.

He rings the bell. The door is promptly answered by a very handsome young man. Who is smiling in the friendliest of manners, and who is wearing shorts, socks, and nothing else. Lawyer Duffy stands for five full seconds—which is really a rather long time under such circumstances—mute.

He finds he cannot take his eyes off the young man's amazingly blue-black hair. How can it be shining, with no sun or light upon it?

To the young man's open expression of disarming welcome, Randolph Duffy hears himself say, "Is my sister at home?" He loves his sister, he has always cared for her, and even this unfathomable encounter will be accepted by him. But he will never forgive himself for having uttered so ridiculous a sentence, and he will never completely forgive her for engineering the scene of the only truly ludicrous moment in his entire life.

*

A busy Saturday for Knoxville.

Rodney pulls up to Kim and Andrea's house in the Victorian neighborhood. This is not to be the last such occasion he enters this locale; nice things can make their way out of the debris of the awful, after all. But his motivation in returning will be quite different, as will be the house itself.

He carefully draws near the curb, recalling and disliking the weakness he had displayed on the previous Friday night. In fairness to him, the resolve he had sought to maintain was of excellent stuff. But he or it had not reckoned on the exceptionally charged power of Andrea that night. He had been a mounted knight with a javelin aimed at a canon. Andrea had won. She had secured from him a promise to elevate their relationship. She had acquired this through a combination of relentless focus upon his freckles and a particularly prolonged pretense of affection following the sex she had forced upon him. Rodney had gone home, debilitated in spirit and in body. It is horrible when someone with a modest but solid base of humanity finds it smashed under his feet.

Every hour since has been nightmarish to him. He knows he must fetch Andrea today, take her to a movie, and offer something in the way of a future to her. But perhaps even good Rodney knows that the rubble of your best self under your feet is still solid, and can be, with a swift move from your foot, a dangerous projectile.

He had remained in the car the other night, honking the horn to alert
Andrea as to his arrival. He repeats the proceedings today. Yet today the
honk of the car horn itself begins the sequence which permits his final
escape, a sequence as quick and as seemingly orchestrated as a fast bank
heist. For today the blare resounds in his own ears, and the Andrea-
induced sogginess between them becomes for his brain, not a dulling
mildew, but a better conduit for electrical impulses.

He looks down at the khaki trousers on his legs, unwilling to let even
his peripheral vision remind him of the fact of Kim inside the house and
of the sad, but courageously challenging, look she had given him when
they had once met. As if to say, Brother, see ye in my eyes what ye know to
be true, draw heart from it, and act. Flee, flee.

So Rodney raises his head, ironically prompted to do so by the memory
he sought to avoid, and by the voltage unleashed with the car horn's brass
call. His left leg twitches, just below the knee. He looks to the house, to
the light behind the living room curtains. He has a sense, admittedly not
of metaphysical origin, of Kim inside. And expectant.

The front door opens by just a sliver; this is the striptease of entrance
Andrea likes to perform under such circumstances. She then appears,
more malignant in the diminution the distance of the yard imparts to her.
She turns her back to lock the door. At that moment Rodney is perfectly
concentrated on the proscenium of the house front, on Andrea's hunched
back, the single light bulb above her, the frame of the place. He is literally
staring wide-eyed at all of it. Including the window to Andrea's right with
the soft glow behind it. Whose curtains now part by a finger's breadth.

Rodney turns to face straight ahead. He does not actually see Kim peer
through the drape, but of course it is her. That it is indisputably her and
not merely a supposition on his part drops the last shoe, as it were. Aware
from the corner of his eye that Andrea is greedily scurrying down the
walkway to him, he then violently unleashes the muscle spasm that had
been chronically afflicting him since the onset of the relationship. He lets
it fly and do with his leg what it will. The impulse wastes no time in

making the most of its host's indulgence, sends a message to a waiting twin in his right arm, and in concert shifts the vehicle out of 'park' and cues his foot to slam on the gas pedal. Flee, he does.

One thing, as he races away into the gray afternoon, away forever from Andrea, and to a rather imminent future: Kim is indeed within the house. But has not gone to the window at all.

Eighteen

A Family Crisis, and a Not Unfamiliar Mishap

Louisa Duffy greets her brother looking much as he has always seen her. Her robe is the same sensible flannel it always is. Her living room as well bears no traces of a world gone mad; the furniture is where it usually is, the drapes are as creamy and as halfway drawn as they customarily are, and the family photographs on the cherrywood credenza retain the slightly askew smiles offered to that alien instrument, the camera, they always present. Not one eyebrow in the lot arches to register distaste. Not one mouth, even that of the sepia Grandmother Duffy, takes the shape of the speechlessly aghast.

In a world that made sense, a thoroughly legal world, Miss Duffy would at least be scarlet of complexion and clutching at the flimsy night-dress inadequately concealing her.

Bob seems to have become one with the air, after admitting Randolph. He is gone. Said Duffy, as yet in the throes of an unthinking stupor, is nonetheless capable of appreciating this single decency, even as the irrationality of the scene implants in his mind the image of the boy striding home, carefree, in socks. He stands in the center of the room as his sister comes to embrace him in her ordinarily business-like way. She is so very much Louisa, so as he ever sees her in his mind and in their daily lives, as to put forth on the scales of the Duffy brain for fast weighing the possibility that he is now in his dotage; that no handsome, nearly nude young man opened the door with the appalling ease of the exceedingly at-home.

"Randolph. Did I know you were coming? I'm sorry."

Duffy's eyebrows rise and his mouth descends, creating a seldom seen expanse of fresh facial territory. He murmurs something neither of them understands.

"Would you like coffee?"

He intends to scan her countenance while confronting her with his own, best courtroom one, the look of dull iron he perfectly keeps in place. He has, as do most other lawyers and all good poker players, reliable experience of the power of an unchanging expression directed at the culpable; sooner or later, the other party breaks. But he finds he cannot perform this well-rehearsed trick. Not on Louisa, not on his baby sister. All he can do, in fact, is stare at her eyes. Which are, astonishingly, holding their own quite nicely. If there is anything to be read into them, it is perhaps a touch of concern.

Suddenly the gorgeously sculpted head of Bob protrudes from the hall, the remainder of his masculine beauty veiled by plaster and paint. "Weez, you know where my sneakers are? They're not in the bedroom."

Never, not in the face of the most shockingly unforeseen revelation from a witness, not at the zenith of a tribute to him at a dinner given by his peers, not even as a teenage Duffy first acquainted with physical desire and its shattering effect on the male frame, has he ever felt so lightheaded, so unsteady on his feet. It is not senility. The boy is right there. His black hair is still tousled with the confessional cowlicks of the recently awakened. And that shining hair is a matter of a yard or two away from the cherrywood credenza and the likeness and power of Grandmother Duffy. Randolph drops his eyes and his head.

"Oh! Louisa. Louisa."

"Did you look under the bed?"

"Oh. Oh, *Louisa!*"

He makes his way to a chair. Miss Duffy is momentarily at a loss; she is unsure if her brother requires assistance, and she knows that Bob does. The former may be all right or may be suddenly ill, but Bob's inability to locate his footwear is not the small affair it may seem. For Louisa knows too, immediately, that Bob must go.

Which, aware as we are of the dreams of Miss Duffy, is fine.

*

Rodney, free. Rodney, flying, fleeing.

He is more exhilirated than he can ever recall being, aware that the wonderful sensation flooding his being is unknown to him because he has never been in a position to escape with his life before. And these are the very things that make life so precious, those close calls: those pianos falling on sidewalks, those head-on collisions averted by an inch, those vile people who almost swallow us.

The Saturday sky's dullness of color is translucently pure, as he careens down the street. Rodney's reverie is electric. It is also extremely short. For he quits the long block of Andrea and Kim's house, turns onto Gibb with no concrete notion of where he is going, and drives into John Grigio.

*

The next day, a Sunday.

Be thankful, Knoxville, that it is Sunday. For you require a great deal of healing.

Randolph Duffy has passed the evening at his sister's apartment. This is as drastic a change in routine as he may very well have ever dared, but circumstances dictate. In this case, they screamed. Hours were needed before Randolph could begin to think and perform again as the Duffy model he customarily is; the shock to his system had in effect shut it down, and rebooting takes a little time in older machines.

And, as Randolph's wiring connected once again to Randolph's impulses, Louisa was there for him. She sat and was silent much of the time, and spoke when he called for answers. These, too, she delivered as gently and as honestly as possible. But convalescence, even that of a single evening, is a curious thing, for the minds of the wounded and the watcher are moving, and moving in directions they usually do not take. Regular existence has been suspended, so the larger issues of the lives concerned are examined in the time which must pass at its own pace. What then results are often fresh insights, and softer outlooks on the landscapes we so unthinkingly tread upon in our non-recuperative days.

Yet there are so many, many roads that we don't pursue. When two people pause to investigate a few, they may still, despite more loving inclinations and stronger desires to be as one with the other, end up miles apart. Randolph Duffy had spent his life caring for Louisa, confident in the correctness of his attentions towards her, confident too in her recognition of them. As she had never ceased suppressing her single carnal need, never doubting that its exposure would destroy her brother. Years of caring from both sides, lifetimes of it, but blind to the other. Thus would it be poetically lovely, but highly unlikely, that shifts in the perception of each would grant to each Duffy purer sight.

By early Saturday evening, Randolph was sufficiently himself to engage in a broken, but at least progressive, dialogue with his sister. By bedtime, he was able to look to the perfunctory matters of being an unexpected houseguest: pyjamas, toothbrushes, message checking at home. By morning, he was not a new man. But he was one who had come to terms with the devastation of the previous day, and in a way–poor Louisa!–completely in keeping with the steadfast and colossally ignorant love he had always held for her.

Poor Louisa? As she prepares coffee, she breathes more easily. Her brother was exposed to the aftermath of her first lustful assignation. This was as regrettable a case of timing as could be conceived. But he is all right, he has slept well, and she dares to hope that their relationship will survive this trauma.

Poor Louisa. It has not occurred to her that Randolph saw the presence of Bob in her home as something other than the handsome residue of an hour's carnality.

Mr. Duffy, respectable in emergency sleepwear, enters the small kitchen of Louisa's apartment. "Morning, Lou."

"Good morning, Randolph. Some eggs?"

He declines eggs, but accepts toast and marmalade. There is something beautifully intimate when two people come together following a break of any kind. Honoring of the unspoken bonds is as directly acknowledged as it ever can be. Not surprising, in the brilliance of such rare light, that the participants are rather clumsy, and hesitate over the most basic actions. Like spreading jam on bread, and looking at one another.

"Lou, I think I should apologize. For coming over like that, yesterday."

"No. No, Randolph. Please don't."

He draws a deep breath; this is the right thing to do. He has been revolving it in his mind for the past twelve hours, and is sure. "You have your own life, after all."

"Oh, Randolph. No, really, I don't."

"Nonsense, Lou."

Miss Duffy goes for more cream. This is amazing. This is wonderful. She is inexpressibly grateful that her brother has come through his emotional ordeal so well, and emerged so charitably. No fool, Louisa Duffy, she decided last night that, should Randolph come out of it at all, she would never again allow such a mischance to happen. There are motels, after all.

Brother and sister sit across from each other at her little wicker table. Coffee steams in mugs, strawberry preserve brightens the minor tableau. Louisa sips, Randolph munches. The moment is one of sibling transcendence.

"So, tell me about Bob."

Miss Duffy's mug stops at a point a few inches south of her lower lip. "Bob?"

"Yes, Lou. Bob. Your...young man."

In suddenly understanding that her brother perceived what he had seen as one post-romantic moment in a relationship of as yet unknown duration, Louisa also is stricken with the fact that she has no subterfuge with which to play along. Dear God. Her brother thinks she is in love with a boy. That was the shock, that was the incomprehensible aspect to the scene he had walked in on. And, steam filling her eyes—the mug remains stationary, poised between worlds—Louisa scrambles to revert to her persona of loving deception. Discarded for twenty minutes out of many, many years.

One would think it would be, then, easy to resume. It is almost impossible.

"Bob."

Randolph, indulgently modern now, actually chuckles. "That's right, Lou. Bob."

"There's...not a lot to say. Randolph."

"Now, I'm sure that isn't the case. Don't be shy, Lou." He reaches across the table and places an affectionate hand on her shoulder. He says meaningfully, "Don't be afraid. You can tell me about it. I'm ashamed that you never thought you could."

Dear God. In her mind Miss Duffy curses the hour she encountered Bob at the hospital, curses his good-natured receptivity to the flagrant advance she astoundingly made, curses her brother's car for not having broken down on the day before.

"He's a very sweet young man, Randolph."

"I'm sure he is, dear. Of course, I hardly spent any *time* with him. But that can be corrected, don't you think?"

"He's very busy, Randolph. He works at the hospital."

Duffy is pleased. There may be little seediness to this affair, after all. Everyone says that a difference of age is of no consequence these days.

"Don't tell me a doctor, Lou? I would've thought…well, a bit young."

"No, not a doctor. Bob is an intern."

Duffy is less pleased. But makes a mental note to obfuscate this minor detail when associates and friends are apprised of his sister's romance.

"Well, that's fine." Louisa Duffy tightens; she can hear what is coming. "So…how long have you been seeing him?"

It does cross her mind that she might now seize this opportunity and reveal the actual situation to her brother. He survived one blow, and may just be stronger than she has ever supposed. But how? How to shatter him all over again? She knows moreover that a large factor in the equanimity she sees sitting across from her table is due to the patina of respectability Duffy reflexively attached to her liaison. Take that away, leave him with nothing but a sister who would be in his eyes, not only wanton, but the instigator of the lewdness…No. This cannot be chanced. As it could not for all those years.

Then, those very years of well-meant duplicity return to Miss Duffy in full force. They come to her, and to her brother's, rescue.

"The thing is, Randolph, I've been seeing Bob for some time now."

"Really, Lou?" Duffy is further abashed at this further testimony to his own inaccessibility as her protector, her big brother.

"Oh, yes. Some time now." She rises, her flannel robe rustling against her chair, and fetches the coffee pot. "About a year."

"Lou. I'm so sorry that you felt you couldn't tell me."

"Hush, Randolph." This is not easy for Miss Duffy; she cannot have him through misguided repentance make it worse. Already, all her control is required to maintain the even pitch of her voice. "Don't blame yourself."

"I do, Lou."

"Well, *don't*. Please. For me."

Duffy is touched by this consideration. So affected, he is as amenable to the ploy she must perpetrate as he ever will be. With love, she carries on.

"What's funny, Randolph, is–well, it's just so *funny*." Duffy's redoubtable eyebrows rise in expectancy. "You caught us on what I think was our last...date."

Duffy is flabbergasted. "No. Really?"

"Yes." She hurries to waylay the imaginary scenarios of rejection, of a slight to his sister's esteem by a callous youth, he will immediately conjure. "He's wonderful, really, and we care for each other."

"Of course you do." The converse is as unthinkable to Duffy as Louisa knew it to be.

"But the age difference...it's just too much, Randolph. I find we have little in common."

"That's too bad, Lou." Duffy, brightening.

"Movies, songs, politics. Everything."

"Naturally, I suppose." Duffy, brighter.

"He's very smart, you know. And great fun. But those differences...we both felt it wasn't working."

Duffy, fully aglow. But let not the wattage of his relief detract from the authentic sorrow he feels for his baby sister's failed romance.

The day gradually changes for Randolph and Louisa Duffy, then, into the garb of all their days together. Small talk once more gathers preeminence in their discourse; lunch is taken at one of the nicer chains on Kingston Pike. Over salads and sandwiches and iced tea, Louisa feels the undercurrents of several distinct reliefs coursing through her. It is astounding. She has gratified at last her physical desire, so long in abeyance. That was rather fun; not precisely as earthshaking as forty-odd years of preparatory imagining would have it, but fun nonetheless. It opened the door for new reveries, in fact, and the waiter who attends to the Duffys today is the first to receive the better educated eye of lustful speculation Miss Duffy will henceforth practice on all members of his tribe.

Better still: her brother knows of this side of her, or at least that sex is within the range of his sister's experience, and is all right. He is not crushed, and she is still a Duffy. She suggests they have dessert today, so celebratory is her mood. Over strudel and a brownie in an avalanche of ice cream, Louisa Duffy reflects that life is as fine as she always suspected it to be.

She is returned to her apartment by early evening, absolutely exhausted; they had used Randolph's car. Who declines the offer to come in for a moment before heading home. Brother and sister then smile sympathetically in amused recognition of the excessive amount of time they have spent together in the past twenty-four hours.

At her door, Randolph hesitates like a clumsy suitor, wanting to say something.

"I've been thinking, Lou."

"Yes, Randolph?" As her big brother, he could never do wrong, even in the fixing up of the awful dates her charitable frame of mind now laughs away. He is especially inviolate, extra wonderful, in her eyes today. She is in fact eager to do something for him, and hopes he is about to frame a request.

"You know, I meet all sorts of men at the office. Lou—" he begins, then chuckles a bit at his former ignorance of her newly revealed predilection in romance, "–they're not all old fogies, either."

Fifty-nine is not very ancient at all. But there are only so many explosions to the system any human can withstand in the space of a day. Miss Duffy is silent. What she is hearing cannot be.

"As a matter of fact, I sometimes lunch with Fielding Pratt. The builder, you know."

Her face remains a mask of suspended disbelief. Which Duffy misinterprets.

"No, no, dear. Not *him*. That won't do, will it, now?"

Somehow, thinks Miss Duffy, the past has come alive again and taken on a truly grotesque form.

"But there's this young chap, very fine boy, who works for them."

Louisa Duffy in that moment washes out to sea, in a manner of speaking. She understands fully well Randolph's future intentions. She wills a smile to form on her face, and kisses her brother farewell. Inside her apartment, she locks the door tight.

Nineteen

Paths Revisited, Paths Trod Anew, and Further Baking

Nearly two months later. This December in Knoxville is penitent and mild, as though to atone for its bitter presence in the previous year.

In the living room of Spite Hall is a foursome linked through chance, deliberate intent temporarily misdirected, mutual regard with mutual affection, and the two aftermaths of two car accidents. As these links are not restricted to mere pairs of the individuals present, the quartet is tied together on an abundance of levels not usually present in the closest of gatherings.

Rene Dacres and Rodney Bourne are hanging ornaments on John's tree. To John's exceedingly dictatorial instruction. He sits in his chair, his good leg terminating with its foot on the hardwood floor, his almost comically unfortunate other leg resting on a massive ottoman. In a thick velvet robe, he thrusts his walking stick in the air to indicate where branches have been neglected. He abruptly chooses and rethinks the ball or miniature toy drum right for the barren spaces, and barks out a series of contradictory orders. He is a holiday tyrant.

In spite of it or because of it, Rene and Rodney do much eye-rolling. They indulge him, the fun lying in the exploitable immobility of their commander.

"Rene."

"Yes, John?" Even in satirical promptness of attention, Rene's fondness for her former boss can be heard.

"Why aren't I seeing Charley-in-the-box?"

"John?"

"Charley-in-the-box. Or Yukon Cornelius, or that idiot doll girl with nothing wrong with her?"

Rodney, precariously perched on a stool with the innate agility of young men and dangling a little sled by a hook, looks from Rene to John. He is lost.

"They're at the restaurant, John. Where they always were."

Rodney asks, "What are they?" The question dissolves in the loving duel taking place between his girlfriend and John.

"That's what I mean." He brings the cane down hard on the floor in despotic parody. "Why didn't you—why didn't *we*—think to get them out of there?"

Rene returns to hanging the clearly uninteresting globe in her hand. "Well, we didn't think of it, that's all."

"*You* didn't think of it, you mean."

Love is so capacious that a million little spites are as nothing to it.

"Yes, John. I didn't think of it."

Rodney makes as one branch and sled, and tries again. "What are you guys talking about?" Rene says nothing but smiles widely with her lips closed tight.

"He doesn't know?" This from John. Rene maintains her smile, twists a metal hook, and still says nothing. "Boy, are you telling me you don't know who Yukon Cornelius is? Can this *be*?"

At that moment Ruth Childress enters from the kitchen. In a slightly dirty cooking apron, and with diamonds catching the candlelight on her fingers and her hair and face done just right for seasonal merrymaking, she appears to be a doll dressed by a child who couldn't quite make up her mind as to her toy's agenda for the day: homemaker, or stylish matron.

"Now, that's one of my favorites. Is it coming on?"

The quartet all in one room, the situation is explained to Mrs.
Childress by Rene, and Rodney gets a rudimentary but highly charged
synopsis of 'Rudolph, the Red-nosed Reindeer' from John Grigio.

*

As is done in both good and poor films, we go back. We retrace the
eight steps of the four in Spite Hall, to better see the increasingly joined
trajectories that brought them together.

Mrs. Childress did indeed keep her appointment with John on that
rather busy Saturday in October. It just didn't transpire as planned by
either of its participants, and certainly not as engineered by Ellen Ansley.

Finding John's house was quite easy for Ruth, given the activity swarm-
ing around it. She had driven halfway up to the corner on which Spite
Hall sits—the occasion was such that she nerved herself to make the trip
alone—when an emergency van deftly skirted her car, raced ahead, and
suddenly stopped. Negotiating the remaining distance, then, at a cautious
five miles per hour, Mrs. Childress became more aware with each yard
gained of what lay at the end of her destination. Or at least she began to
take in a nightmarish interpretation of a scene too terribly familiar to her.

For there was John Grigio, on his back, on the chilly ground just past
his oak tree. From the gesturings of the medics hovering over him, it
appeared that his left leg was badly hurt. Again. Clearly not a medic but
obviously belonging to the scene was a young blonde man, standing with
his arms folded, and stunned of expression.

If greedy relations are the immediate attendants upon death, para-
medics are the less avaricious but equally unfailingly present handmaidens
of crisis. Whatever their training and irregardless of the accent in which it
is given, they appear in no time like loud phantoms, moving with identical and well-rehearsed rapidity in any locale, skirting the ambulatory main
players of the scene. In no time at all John was scooped up onto a

stretcher, slid into the van's rear like a pie going into a warm oven, and swept off. To Baptist hospital. Once again.

Two police cars occupied the accident landscape, as well. These remained after the victim had been removed, and the four officers belonging to them alternately pulled out notepads, re-entered their cars to provide data to the station, asked series of questions to both Rodney Bourne and Mrs. Childress, and generally comported themselves with that unsettling air of satisfaction policemen often manifest when something wrong has occurred and they are needed.

How did it happen? They asked this of Rodney with no outward sign of yet knowing that he was responsible, despite that fact's rather glaring presence. Rodney responded with all the honesty in his being, which is substantial. So without artifice is the boy, so unencumbered with mechanisms of self-protection when the culpability is his, that his account gave the police pause. It was not usual in their experience to hear a guilty party so objectively outline his guilt. It was strange to record an accident as told by the perpetrator without its being punctuated by excuses, by suddenly conjured extenuating factors, feverishly introduced.

As Rodney carefully recounted the circumstances, Mrs. Childress took it in less passively than did the gentlemen scribbling it down. With each successive action related–there were few to tell, as the entire collision had been as simple as a simple sentence–Ruth empathized more and more with the blonde boy unknown to her. By the tale's conclusion, she had made up her mind to ensure that this young man would be all right. He would in fact drive the two of them to the hospital.

*

Hospitals have short memories, and very little in the way of a sense of humor.

The few at Baptist who recalled John's similarly occasioned stay with them found this repeated incident unexciting, and certainly unworthy of commentary. When initial treatment required the answering of basic questions, many of which pertained to the history of the damaged limb, no one seemed at all intrigued by the coincidence of it. Almost exactly one year later, and the same leg is hurt by the same means, and nothing. No bad jokes, no amazed shakes of heads, nothing. By the time he was placed in a small room—it was not 232, thankfully; that would have taken the episode to a sphere of reoccurrence too uncanny—John had come to the conclusion that cumulative fear of any type of malpractice litigation had erased whatever humor these people had once been allowed to professionally exercise.

What is the diagnosis, this time around? A fracture, yes. The old woman who wielded the x-ray clicker in October of 1996 still held her remote and her job, and her fingers were no more adroit in the disrobing of her clients than they had been in October of 1996. A doctor other than Ring Perkey looked thoughtfully at the scans. By early evening, he was prepared to talk to John.

"Interesting break."

"Is it?"

"Yes. Just over the old one. Whoa, boy."

" 'Whoa, boy?' "

"Sorry. Yes. Over the old. But clean, nice and clean."

John took this as a personal compliment. "Doctor, how long are we looking at?"

"Oh, it'll be a while. The bone should start making sticky stuff—you just winced, are you all right?—within the week. But I wouldn't sign up for any 10K runs, if I were you."

John smiled wanly. Then this orthopedist came as close to actually referring to the unlikelihood of the situation as anyone would.

"You really need to stop doing this, son."

*

Spite Hall in December, again.

Mrs. Childress wipes her hands on her apron. The apron is of holiday design, with berries and holly on the lap of it. With jewelry glittering and thusly attired, little Mrs. Childress is herself a Christmas ornament.

The scandal of the moment is that Rodney is unfamiliar with the annually televised claymation saga of Rudolph. John, relentlessly inquisitive with subjects dear to him, wants to know how this can be.

"I guess we just never watched it, John."

"Charlie Brown? Did your people"—the sneer is both deliberate and feigned—"condescend to watch Charlie Brown?"

"Sure."

"The *Grinch?*"

"Absolutely." Rodney, still poised standing on the stool, strains to place tinsel within the upper reaches of the tree. "And 'Frosty', too."

"Well, then." John looks to Rene, then to Ruth, and speaks with the mild hubris of having solved a particularly baffling riddle. "That's your problem."

"Who would like cookies?" Mrs. Childress chimes in with this modestly, and Rene exposes a waving hand from behind a patch of pine. Rodney nods like a freckled puppy. And no one seems terribly interested in John's solution.

"Where I come from, you had your Frosty families and your Grinch-C. Brown-Rudolph households." No one disputes this, but the conformity may be due more to gingerbread than to educated assent. "I don't want to embarrass you, Rodney, but the better homes *did not watch* Frosty."

Rodney is unembarrassed. His open-eyed and ruddy-faced acceptance of this assessment from John, in fact, might lead an outsider to reconsider the respective arguments against the Snowman's television adventure. Ruth sits on the sofa, periodically lifting the plate of baked stars and green triangles up in the air as an offering to the elevated members of the company. She is delighted to be the source of nourishment for these twin laborers. Then she remembers: she has a pie in the oven.

*

"This is all very strange."

This observation made by Ruth Childress in the waiting area of Baptist's emergency room was one which can hardly have been new to the environment. Rodney had just returned from the windows whence updated information regarding those deeper within the hospital's confines may, by chance and usually only by chance, be obtained.

"She said, they don't know anything yet."

"Thank you, dear. I rather thought they wouldn't, just yet."

"Well. *I'd* like to know something." This had been begun by Rodney as an impatient declaration, but he is too good-mannered to give the words such a thrust. So it came out as wistful. Coincidentally enough, it was a voiced expression of the curiosity John's first accident of the year before had drawn out in him.

"Now, Rodney. These things take time."

"Right."

The old woman and the young man sat, then, for nearly an hour. Unassuming both, they had each instinctively elected to sit together in a corner, removed from the busier aisles of more pressing needs and more pressing friends and relatives. So distanced, the intimacy between them moved even more inward. Shared catastrophes are said to ignite instant connections between people. Two souls who first encounter one another violently somehow bypass the requisite years of acquaintance; the many layers obscuring true character are immediately exposed and, if each can embrace the other, embracing takes place.

No, the calamity in which Rodney and Ruth played parts was not of a truly explosive kind. But the groundwork had already been laid, unbeknownst to them. Each had a history with John Grigio. And—surely an effective substitute for the bonding circumstance of a genuinely extraordi-nary first meeting–their individual histories with John mirrored one another reversely, as in a funhouse. As Rodney was the second to actually strike John with an automobile, Ruth Childress could empathize to a degree highly precise. Support groups include those who hug one another in united despair of having inflicted vehicular damage upon a person. How many, even in that rarified sphere of angst, can claim the same victim?

They sat, and spoke in whispers. What they actually said to each other can be easily surmised; much of it revolved around the very coincidence of their being together. The rest can be determined from the very end of their conversation, before word came to them that John would be all right.

"I was so looking forward to our seeing one another today, too."

"I'm sure," Rodney assented. "I'm sorry."

"You musn't be sorry for *that*, dear. Goodness. Isn't it bad enough that we've taken turns in striking him down?"

It may have been the phraseology of it rather than the sentiment, but both started to laugh.

"This is going to sound strange," Rodney began, "but I've been inter-ested in what happened to you both last year."

"Well. It was an interesting situation, I suppose."

Rodney looked Mrs. Childress fully in the face. "Not just a car acci-dent, you mean."

"Oh, no. Hardly just that."

"That he waited for it to happen."

"Yes."

"I thought so. People said so, anyway."

The past year has wrought subtle changes to the fiber of Ruth Childress. She is capable now of perceiving things formerly unseen, or sus-pected and left alone by her. Now, she is politely but firmly dismissive.

"Oh, *people*. What can they know about it?" There is a long and com-fortable silence. Ruth ends it. "I was thinking, Rodney: why don't you see if you can call that young woman from John's restaurant?"

Then, as if in tribute to the grace of the old woman and young man together, the unthinkable happened. A nurse sought them out, and told them what they needed to know.

*

As for Mr. Grigio, in his few days at Baptist: no extravagant prose is called for to convey his sensibility. Take the surreal perceptions brought about through dramatic injury, heavy medication and alien surroundings, and square them.

When he periodically awoke, he not unnaturally believed himself to be in the exact situation of the year before. Which, to the logical pathways of his relaxed brain, rendered the previous twelve months a dream. There had been no monthly pies, no stolen afternoon in Krutch Park with Rene, no Miss Marchbanks—and, if anything more could lend the past reality the aspect of a dreamscape, that redoubtable woman's presence could—and no fine settlement from the Childress insurance people.

But something was not sitting right in this neural attempt to sort out what had befallen him. Several things, in fact, were wrong. He could so clearly see Mrs. Childress' face behind a windshield, yet some bizarre brushstroke of his mind persisted in adding freckles to her face. He could recall his apartment quite accurately, yet could not place in its interior or exterior the gargoyle which kept intruding into the mental image. Most baffling of all to his senses and his fragmented memory was reliving the moment of being hit on Clinch and Gay and seeing, inches from his face, the trunk of an oak tree. He could see ants, even, going through their frantic business.

When the actual facts of the matter cohered within his mind, the other worldly element of them did not necessarily depart. A ridiculous coincidence seen through refreshed eyes is still a ridiculous coincidence. On the afternoon of his second day there, genuine confusion had already given way to abstract musing and speculative reflection. Preeminent in John's thoughts was a peculiar relief. He had been terribly hurt through his own stubborn spite a year ago, and he was severely injured again. But he had in no way courted this latest fracture. On his small lawn, he had been momentarily drawn to what appeared to be ancient initials carved into the side of his oak tree. And, for no real reason at all, and assuredly for nothing with even the barest trace of spite about it, he had suddenly felt an impulse to step back and take in his whole property; as his guest, Mrs. Childress, would see it from the street. He recalled vividly his desire that it be pleasing to her. Then there was the car, and the briefest possible taking in of that boy's face behind the wheel. Two eyes huge in alarm in a sea of freckles.

Nonetheless: it was purely an accident. Or it was preordained that so unquestionable a mischance should occur to him, that he might see how his original sanctioning of damage to himself was not the folly anyone would claim it to be. For it now appeared that life could exercise a spiteful twist, as well as any spiteful man could. Maybe, John thought, it was all a singular sort of war: drawn out, broken up by long truces, but never fully abandoned. And composed of enemies greater than townspeople with poor driving skills.

Things make their way into focus. We are confident that we have a grasp on what was perplexing. In these times and at many, many others, we are reminded that certainty is a gift attached to a long string in somebody else's hand.

It was on that second day that John realized, as a smoker will, that he hadn't had a cigarette in two days. Drugs had blurred the hard edge of addiction, but renewed clarity carried with it old vice. And, just as this craving spurred in him the seeds of plans to assuage it, the door to his room opened and Bob stepped in.

Throughout John's evident stupefaction, Bob was himself. He was the same, good-natured intern John had known a year ago. There was no single thing in his manner or actions to betray the awkwardness of his visit to John's home, the awfulness of his eviction from there as a presumed hustler.

As a matter of fact, he joked. "You book this suite every year, sir?"

Resolution, thankfully, does not hold up when it is comprised of mistaken intent. That is a kind of failsafe in human relations, and an immeasurably valuable one, too. Greater resolves crumble as well, but that is a different and sadder story, and not applicable here.

John smiled in response. He should have been aloof, politely cold, to Bob. But, human, he had within him now the clear-sighted sense of perspective commonly witnessed in people recently hit by cars. This is not to say that he had suddenly revised his assumption of just what had brought Bob to Spite Hall that day; rather, it was simply unimportant. To John's credit, he held to this fresh opinion without first seeing Bob as a means to a smoke.

"Listen," he said, "I owe you an apology."

Bob was generously uninterested. "Nah. Don't worry about it, man."

"No. Really. It's been a strange year." This was meant to emerge as more explanatory than it in fact came out. Yet young people like Bob are well used to vagaries of speech; if the sentiment is understood, they need little exactitude of expression.

"Not a problem. You comfortable?"

"Thanks, I'm fine." Bob moved about the room, replacing used implements with sterile replacements. The mood within the space then called out for more, and more with candor, and candor with an edge to it.

"So you're *not* a gay hustler?"

John was right. Not in his initial view of Bob as predatory, but in blatantly referring to what he was suddenly quite sure had been his own misapprehension of the young man. Bob broke out into a smile so brilliantly open that his normally stunning looks were amplified to a state absolutely unfair to the rest of the mortal world.

"Last time I checked, no."

The two men were then in a state of perfect ease with one another. Almost as the nearly identical driving mishaps of Rodney Bourne and Mrs. Childress opened an exceptionally clear and wide channel for their humanities to meet, so did the past year's gaffe of John's interpretation of

Bob's financial blues-crying now dissolve layers of the clumsy stages gone through before genuine knowledge of another is had.

This happy meeting of human natures could not have transpired, of course, without the otherwise unbearable fact of Bob's being as innocent as he was handsome.

An even broader smile illuminates the beauty of Bob. Something has occurred to him.

"I could let you meet one of my girlfriends. But you probably wouldn't believe it." And, as John furrows his brow in mild puzzlement, Bob adds: "Bet you're needing a cigarette, about now."

*

Alice Ann Dacres' eyes had never taken in so much, so quickly. They darted in every corner of Rene's room, and never ceased searching for more. This might have been construed by someone who knew her well as symptomatic of agitation of spirit, no matter how seemingly serene her exterior. By someone like, say, Rene.

But Rene continued packing. There was nothing more to say, unless her aunt was willing to disclose the anguish her casual comments were failing to adequately conceal. This, four days after John's second pardon from his Baptist incarceration, in mid-October.

"You know, honey, I can bring on over anything you need."

"I know. I just don't want you to have to take the trouble."

Her hands at her shapely waist, one leg provocatively set with its knee resting upon the edge of Rene's bed, Alice Ann uttered the sound commonly known as a 'raspberry', and says, "*Trouble?*" Thusly spoken, the word defied its speaker's intent and seemed to serve instead as an alert to Alice Ann's internal state.

"I don't have much, thank God," said Rene, folding a sweater.

And will have precious little more, thought Alice Ann, if you pursue a course of throwing your life away upon a homosexual.

"Besides, Alice Ann, I don't even know how long it'll be for. Like I told you. So it's not like I need everything I own." Rene was careful not to use John's name, if it could be avoided. The circumstance of this temporary move had been explained as gently as possible to her aunt; the perfectly good reasoning of her staying in the house of a friend to help out as she could, as well as the unimpeachably correct arrangements for her accommodation within it. But it was best not to fan the flame. Whatever that flicker was inside of Alice Ann, unnecessary reminders of just who the impaired friend was would serve as a spattering of fuel to it.

"Not too long, I hope, honey. Gee, but I'm gonna miss you." Coquettishly, Alice Ann drew a handkerchief from the pocket of her housedress and dabbed one eye.

Rene saw the gesture for the theatrical silliness it was and, being Rene, saw everything underneath it as well. So she walked around the bed and hugged her aunt. The fifth hug, in fact, since the news had been broken two days before.

"Alice Ann. You know you'll be fine. You can even have your friends over for cards without worrying about me. Anything you like."

"Oh, I know, dear. Of *course*. Carolyn…" She paused dreamily here. The bizarre social duel between the two women of Sterling Realty had persisted throughout the past year, and might very well outlive its own combatants, as Yorks and Lancastrians went to their graves only briefly interrupting the War of the Roses. The day before, in fact, Alice Ann had tried out a new weapon. She had sashayed to Carolyn's desk and placed before her the reality of her impending solitude in the house on Pickett Avenue, along with the outrageous suggestion that Carolyn stop on by some evening. If medals were awarded for such things, a *croix de guerre* should have been pinned to Alice Ann's apricot jacket. For Carolyn, customarily the sought-after and thusly more puissant antagonist, was left speechless.

"Yes, Carolyn, whoever you like," Rene contributed.

"Don't you worry about me, honey." This, naturally enough, to mean: I am horrified that you don't see how your actions are wounding me.

Rene scanned the room, searching for something indistinct but perhaps forgotten.

"And it's not like you're going to the ends of the earth."

"No. Not at all." Rene was still distracted. So Alice Ann, slighted emotionally by this greater interest in an unseen scarf or shirt, came as close to making her move as she could. She wanted to be courageous enough to sit Rene down and tell her candidly that this proposed arrangement was absurd. That John Grigio had no interest in her at all, save as a convenience. That she, Rene, may in fact be exposed to all sorts of obscene and unnatural situations, and that none of it was remotely worthwhile for a pretty girl who had wasted plenty of time as it was on a homosexual restaurant manager with a limp.

What she in fact said was, "Rene. You're sure this is the right thing to do?"

"Alice *Ann*. I'm sure."

Thus did Alice Ann Dacres, through what she would later on berate herself for as weakness, a failure to perform an essential duty for her niece, render it easier for Rene to achieve the happiness she herself was quite sure could never be had by so ludicrous a sacrifice.

*

There will be people in Andrea's future, chiefly of temporary acquaintance, who will hear how an old roommate contrived to steal her boyfriend. How this evil roommate undermined what may well have been the great love of Andrea's life. But these stories will be spinned in places like California and Florida, where the wealth of fictional histories their citizens display like trophies will take in her tragedy as the flimsy tin statuette it is. It will be accepted, but there is little comfort from a warm hug in a room full of mannequins, and no satisfaction at all to the sociopath.

Kim Stritch saw in fact a bit less of Rodney Bourne than Andrea did on that last aborted date; the screeching of his tires brought her to the window and, as she was inside the house and thusly yards more removed from

the actual getaway than Andrea, the glimpse of car she had was less. And
neither girl ever saw Rodney again.

In early December, as Rene had assumed the easy familiarity of John's
house and Mrs. Childress had become a not unexpected visitor, Andrea was
booted out of her own. Kim had of course dreaded the moment of informing her of the upcoming eviction, but had steeled herself to it with all the
resolve she was able to command. This was largely due to Rodney's escape.
His daring stayed within her, as a beacon. It could be done.

"I have to move *out?*"

"Yes." Kim was about to say, 'I'm sorry', but resisted the civility.

"God. I don't *believe* this."

"Believe it."

"You *know*, I don't have anywhere to *go*." Andrea's martyrdom might
have carried more conviction, had her eyes flashed a little less ferocity.

Kim was serenely inflexible. She was also astonished at how serene she
felt. It wasn't nearly as horrid as she had anticipated. And she kept in the
forefront of her mind the sound of screeching tires and the blurry image of
the back of a blonde head.

"I'm sure that's not true. You're always talking about how your friends
want you."

"Yeah, but like *this?* No *warning?*"

Kim glowed. "I didn't know your friends needed much warning." Oh,
this could even be a little fun, Kim thought. But was careful not to overdo
it. Simple, she had told herself. Simple, short, and done.

"Tonight," she said, and left Andrea's bedroom. Once again, it is a
shame that no one was present to see Andrea alone, just then. Her small
hands were fists, and her small frame heaved, and her teeth clamped down
hard on her lower lip. Circuitry spewed sparks within her brain; breathing
was hard and fast, little gusts through her nostrils. Someone would pay.

Unnecessary vow! Someone always pays, with an Andrea. But maybe
the vengeful determination diffused her agitation just enough. For, given

all the physical signs she manifested, she really ought to have exploded into bits that hour. Really, she should have.

Twenty

Evening Repose

The remains of an excellent turkey occupy shelf space in John Grigio's refrigerator, along with portions of attendant dishes. Other areas of the kitchen bear other traces of a feast enjoyed hours before: tins of Christmas cookies violated for their more preferred contents, then resealed; an inch of coffee still undrunk in the pot, with strictly seasonal condiments of cinnamon and whipped cream beside it; and almost a half of a pie on the stove, covered in the domestic tinsel of aluminum foil.

Mrs. Childress has gone home. The party had in fact broken up an twenty minutes ago, around nine. Rodney had gallantly carried to her car her special cooking implements, although not all; in a gesture rich with meaning for all concerned, Ruth Childress decided it more prudent to leave her favorite big wooden fork and spoon set, and two of the old tempered glass pie pans she has had forever, with John.

Her departure cued Rodney's. More precisely, Mrs. Childress' impending exit from the scene, with the delays inherent in any elderly woman's leavetaking, gave Rene and Rodney the wonderful opportunity to gracefully slip away into the kitchen and exchange goodbyes of a more intimate, if not more affectionate, kind. The entire breaking-up of the small party was a sort of modern ballet, as such things are when every participant is wholly at ease with every other. It is a rare choreography.

John sinks back into his chair now, grinning, as Rene picks up his ash-tray and a few empty glasses. Nat King Cole is singing 'Little Town of Bethlehem' faintly, and better than it may ever have been sung.

"Yes?" she inquires, her pretty head off to one side.

He looks at her fully. "I was just thinking. Firelight becomes you."

She rolls her eyes. Living with John has taught her much in the way of his twists of speech and harmless digressions.

"Firelight," she dryly replies, "becomes everyone. Even you. What were you thinking, really?"

He searches. She can see him straining a bit behind his mildly fur-rowed brow.

"It's far too dumb."

"All right, then." Rene carries the soiled items to the kitchen, John's not seriously injured eyes following her. She will reappear, of course, and shortly; the spousal rhythms the two had long established at Garamond's transferred quite easily into Spite Hall. When she returns, it is with a fresh drink for John and the last of the coffee for herself.

Rene relaxes onto the sofa and cradles her mug on her lap.

"You know," John slowly draws out, "you could *press* me for what I was thinking."

She is the essence of post-holiday-dinner lassitude, a Norman Rockwell for a magazine cover: feet up, Christmas apron on, bangs limp. The whipped cream on her coffee subtly adds a touch of specificity to the portrait.

"Ohhh...that's fine." One person can learn a great deal in the way of toy sword fencing, in just a month or two. "I don't want to pry."

"How considerate."

"Besides, you'll tell me anyway."

"For an *au pair*, you're pretty sure of yourself." *Au pair*, fac totum, amanuensis. John liked employing these antediluvian descriptions in ref-erence to the vague purpose Rene fulfilled in his little house. He liked the contrast of their grandeur to their small, Knoxvillian life. Rene liked that he liked them, and never asked for definitions.

"No," he decided. "I don't believe I will."

But we will.

When the last of the ice had clinked in the glass Rene removed, John was suddenly reminded of his family, his parents. This in turn sparked more general thoughts of family, a not unlikely sequence in the aftermath of a holiday dinner. And it struck him that his good fortune was not just good, but extraordinarily so. A leg broken twice, a limp he would always have. That was nothing, he considered. To have gained what he had gained seemed so bountiful that the injuries paled. People suffer crippling disasters all the time and come away with nothing but a diminution of what they earlier had. The value of his own life as it now was called out, in his wary mind, for greater offerings.

Nat King Cole sang, 'O, Holy Night'. Rene had her eyes shut in dreamy repose. Was she thinking of Rodney? John hoped so. Had little Mrs. Childress regretted leaving as early as she had? Very likely and John Grigio, not spitefully, rather hoped for that as well. For such a regret would confirm what he already knew full well to be true: that he had stumbled onto the best parts of life through one, and then another, calamity. A year ago he had defiantly set it all in motion, wanting nothing more than to dangerously make a stand. But he had fallen onto the hood of a car and into a deeper hold of life.

If Rodney was indeed in Rene's thoughts, he was occupying the more surreal landscape of dream. She was lightly snoring. John watched her as a parent does a dozing child, with satisfaction in the rest being taken and a ready eye to see that it goes undisturbed.

Who sets these courses? Believer or pragmatist, they must be guided somehow, for it is unreasonable to suppose that accidents can settle into such patterns of rightness. Nor can we think that the rightness is engineered by even obscure parts of ourselves, for the forms it can take are often unthinkable to us. Rene and Rodney together, John as only a friend to both; never, even in his most selfless wishes for her happiness, could such a scenario have occurred to him. Never would he have once entertained the possibility that such an outcome would be in fact the best thing he could wish for. But then, he had not ever foreseen the having of friends. Not until months after the first break to his leg.

The ice tinkles, Nat King Cole repeats his Christmas repertoire. Rene sniffles in her sleep and makes an insentient and missed swipe at her nose. In his own little apartment, Rodney is looking for a receipt; the present he had chosen for Rene, he now thinks, is far from good enough and must be replaced. In her own kitchen, Ruth Childress is mixing a digestive aid into a tumbler of water. She is thinking that she will set aside more time for Ellen Ansley. She has not been ignoring her by any means. But Ruth's increased visits to Spite Hall–she has been apprised of the name, and all its meanings–have naturally enough curtailed her ordinary social calendar. And Mrs. Ansley may just harbor a touch of envy, that her dear friend is so frequently and unpatronizingly welcomed by a coterie of youth.

This night, too, Louisa Duffy consults a new addition to her life: an appointment book. She is tickled anew each time she opens it; that she, volunteer at the library, soulmate to none, should require such a thing! But she does, and tonight she is careful to use the red pen to indicate those nights and hours in which she will be Randolph's sister; the black to mark her library time; and the mercifully erasable pencil to draft potential assignations.

On the next day, a manager from the downtown Sir Speedy office will make a first payment on a diamond ring. The woman who will be his fiancee, Miss Marchbanks, will shriek upon seeing it—that the shriek itself creates no revulsion in the hearer of it, in fact, has much to do with the blossoming of the romance—accept it, and shortly afterward ensure that her future husband knows her career is not one she is prepared to abandon. The associates of Gilley, French and Sweet will embrace her in her good fortune and take solace, not in the faithful Marchbanks' determination to remain with them, but in her age being prohibitive of child-bearing.

Kimberly Stritch will forget Andrea Cornell. It will not happen for a good ten years, but that it will happen at all is something.

Back inside John Grigio's house, Nat King Cole is reprising 'O, Holy Night'. John wonders if the reprise of his own action, the unpremeditated strike from Rodney a year after the less ordinary run-in with Mrs. Childress, was necessary to bring together the harmony now present in all their lives. He will not of course ever know. But we are reminded of a claim not explained, earlier in these pages. To wit: what else was remarkable about John, as once suggested? That real joy could exist for him in the joy of others near him. Is that so very remarkable in anyone? We will not say. To imply such would be cynical. But it is certainly not a joy one would look to find within a spiteful man.

John sets his drink down, knowing without knowing that, very soon, he will be asleep in his chair. And, outside, a red felt hat with a white cotton band at the hem of it and a white cotton ball on its crown is tied around the granite chin of a gargoyle.

**

About the Author

Mr. Mauro currently lives and works in Knoxville, Tennessee.

Printed in the United States
31620LVS00003B/47